Fidelity

Michael Redhill is the author of *Martin Sloane*, winner of the Commonwealth Writers Prize for Best First Book for the Canada/Caribbean region. He has published five poetry collections, most recently *Light-crossing*, and written numerous plays, the most recent of which, *Building Jerusalem*, was a finalist for the 2001 Governor General's Award. Michael Redhill is the publisher and one of the editors of the literary magazine *Brick*.

'[A] superb collection of stories . . . Fabulously ambiguous, open and intimate analyses of the integrity, or not, of certain kinds of longing. The locales and frames . . . might be daily material, but are dissected with a dark humour, a keen ability to unsettle and a startling insight that lifts them well clear of the field . . . At their most acute, and several are masterpieces of the form, these chamber dramas of rupture and shift bear comparison with the best of Raymond Carver and James Salter. Like their's, Redhill's own fidelity to the pursuit of sometimes difficult truths is never in doubt.' *Time Out*

'An impressive collection . . . Time and again, Redhill shows how real life gets in the way of the best-laid plans . . . There is much in these stories of the studied lyricism and poignancy that made *Martin Sloane* such pleasurable reading, but here Michael Redhill has added humour and a refreshing acknowledgement of the absurd.' *TLS*

'A voice that is pure Bernard Malamud . . . You approach each tale with a growing anticipation of angst . . . Then Redhill trumps one's expectation, producing a blindingly comic marvel . . . Bitter sweet magic . . . a beautifully crafted, if sometimes baleful collection.' *Scotland on Sunday*

'Redhill's stories are pretty disturbing, with lyrical flourishes and some penetrating insights . . . Redhill packs a hell of a punch. As someone once remarked of Sonny Liston: "He hurts when he breathes on you".' *Guardian*

'A writer who profoundly understands how we are shaped by the accumulations of our lives and yet how change might suddenly come upon us . . . An absorbing and unusual talent . . . Redhill is a writer of depth and breadth . . . There is much unsettling sadness here, but much satisfying exploratory richness too. The prose, never too overtly poetic, is often exquisite, catching a life in the sudden illumination of an image.' *Scotsman*

Also by Michael Redhill

Martin Sloane

Fidelity

Stories

Michael Redhill

arrow books

Published in 2005 by Arrow Books

1 3 5 7 9 10 8 6 4 2

Copyright © Michael Redhill 2004

Michael Redhill has asserted his right under the
Copyright, Designs and Patents Act, 1988 to be identified
as the author of this work

First published in the United Kingdom in 2004
by William Heinemann

Arrow Books
The Random House Group Limited
20 Vauxhall Bridge Road, London SW1V 2SA

Random House Australia (Pty) Limited
20 Alfred Street, Milsons Point, Sydney,
New South Wales 2061, Australia

Random House New Zealand Limited
18 Poland Road, Glenfield
Auckland 10, New Zealand

Random House (Pty) Limited
Endulini, 5a Jubilee Road, Parktown 2193, South Africa

The Random House Group Limited Reg. No. 954009

www.randomhouse.co.uk

A CIP catalogue record for this book
is available from the British Library

Papers used by Random House are natural, recyclable products
made from wood grown in sustainable forests. The manufacturing
processes conform to the environmental regulations
of the country of origin

ISBN 0 09 945509 9

Printed and bound in Great Britain by
Cox & Wyman Ltd, Reading, Berkshire

For our friends in Kalamazoo

There is the pull of the will and of love,
wherein appear the worth of everything
to be sought, or to be avoided.

ST. AUGUSTINE

Contents

MOUNT MORRIS

Once a year, when he came through town, Tom Lumsden stopped in on his ex-wife and she'd make him dinner and usually he'd stay the night. He looked forward to his visits, with their surfeit of the familiar, and it made him feel like the love that had brought them together still existed between them somehow. It was more than a memory, but less than a presence: a tune they could still hum.

When they'd lived together in Johnstown, in Pennsylvania, they owned the camera supply store there, and although the population was less than 25,000, the town had a campus of the U of Pittsburgh, and every fall a new crop of freshmen would move through. Some of them had cameras, or *photographic needs*, and they'd be a fresh influx of customers for the time they lived in the town. Frosh week was the best week for business, since a few fathers around with sons or daughters would punctuate their these-are-the-best-years-of-your-life speeches with a new camera. Then, at the end of the academic year, there'd be the graduates and *their* gifts. To some of these kids he'd sold two outfits in a four-year period. He liked thinking of himself as a family business, and he and Lillian were often on a first-name basis with their customers, even if they came in only once or twice a year.

They married in '88, when they were both twenty-five, and came out to live in Johnstown, where Tom had bought the camera store from George Lurie with an inheritance. Tom and Lillian had grown up in and near cities, but they adjusted quickly to life in a small town. Lurie's (they kept the name) was the sponsor of a local bantam ballteam that couldn't hit, catch, or run, but the stands would fill up with parents and townies and everyone would cheer these Lurie's Johnstown Shutterbugs. Tom donated the group shots to the teams in the county and neighbouring towns that could fetch up a dozen or so twelve-year-olds and field a team, and over the few years that he and Lillian were together there, he took the team portraits for Altoona and Bedford, and all the little places in between, and that was how he found out he had some small aptitude for arranging groups and getting them to look in the same direction. So when he and Lillian split, he sold the shop and made the sideways move over into portraiture. All that time he'd been selling the raw material without knowing he'd had any touch of the artist himself.

They'd split over a difference that they always knew had been there: Lillian thought he would come around to having kids, and he figured that once she had a house and neighbours and a couple of dogs she'd think twice about cashing it all in for a chance with someone else. But they'd both been wrong. Tom said the reason he had his inheritance at twenty-five was because his dad had worked himself to death in his hardware store keeping a family of six clothed and fed, and he, Tom, wasn't going to do that to himself. "This is a deal-breaker," he'd put it to Lillian, and she had to admit that the deal was broke. She didn't want the store, so he took what he needed out of it for his new career—a Rolleiflex, a backscreen, a tripod, two lamps, a backflash, and a tripwire—sold it, and gave her the money. He took the car and started visiting schools and junior sports teams throughout the state, and after a few years, spread out some into Ohio, as well as New York and New Jersey.

That was twelve years ago, and every year, he kept a date with Lillian, coming through Johnstown, then later Elmira, New York, and now Mount Morris, which was where Lillian's mother lived. Neither he nor Lillian had remarried, although he'd had his relationships and he imagined she'd had hers as well, since she was a pretty woman, and smart, and looked thirty although she was thirty-eight. She told him in a letter (she wrote sometimes; he didn't) that when she turned thirty-seven you'd think all of her was practically teenaged, except for if she was on a diving board in a bikini and you were standing in line behind her. Then you'd know. When he read that, he could hear her laugh that high, sudden laugh of hers.

Now that she was in Mount Morris, and had been there for the better part of five years, he was finding their visits more and more difficult. They were often nostalgic or sometimes even a little bitter. From Lillian's point of view, there was hardly any sense in staying split up, since she'd never had kids and now it was almost too late. Their last two visits, he'd opted not to stay over, saying he had to be in some town a long drive away, when really it was her talking about them like that, as if the past was something that lay dormant and could be reactivated by mutual agreement. He knew that going back for these visits, with this kind of unresolved feeling between them, meant he was sort of using her. But this year he intended to settle everything for good.

He called her from Geneseo, a little town just a few miles to the north of hers, and said he'd be there in time for supper. The shoot in two of Geneseo's high schools took up all of the morning and most of the afternoon. Making his living from school portraiture had turned out to be the most sensible decision for him: all he had to do was risk a couple hundred dollars in film, and four or five boxes of envelopes he'd had made up special, and the rest of it was counting money. It had even gotten to the point that he no longer engaged a printer back in Pennsylvania to make the packages of eight-by-tens and wallet photos. The technology had come so far that if a town was big enough to have a mini-mall with a one-hour photo, all he had to do was go there and give them the negs. And if, in any of the regular stops he made, there was more than one place to develop photos, he'd auction the job off. It was obviously the largest order of the year for any of these small-town shops.

He'd even come to enjoy the continuity of returning to schools, seeing how some of the kids he'd photographed the previous years were growing up. He had boxes full of headshots, and he sometimes recognized the faces as they grew older a year at a time. (The samples that he gave to parents were stamped PROOF ONLY to make it impossible to keep them as wallet snaps.) In Geneseo, he remembered at least a dozen of the kids in the two schools and remarked to himself how much they had changed. Some had grown taller, some fatter, while others had obviously found sports and their little stick-like bodies had thickened with muscle. Still others just seemed older: their faces spoke of home lives that had seen no improvement in the intervening time. It surprised him how much those tired and dour faces upset him, as if by returning to their hometowns each year, he was doing nothing less than recording the inevitability of their declining fortunes. He worried that some of his photos could one day be used in newspapers to record bad tidings—these smiling photos, which always seemed faded and misused once transmitted through newsprint, sometimes made him feel that his work had the potential to be the unhappy ending of someone else's story.

He drove south from Geneseo and to the edge of the national park where Mount Morris was. It wasn't much of a mount, just a faint swelling in the fields. As he had the year before, he stopped right before getting into town and went into a local dining room where a lot of single men ate alone, and he sat down at the bar and had a Rolling Rock. After being by himself for months at a time, he would have to pause before going to see Lillian, to collect the bits of himself that she knew best. He'd always been a light-hearted, jokey guy with her, picking her up out of the dips and dark spots she sometimes fell into. A nice guy, the kind your mother would want you to end up with. Even though, at his centre, he wasn't that kind of guy at all. He was more like Lillian than he'd ever let on.

"You come back to take my photo, honey?" said the woman behind the bar. She'd served him his last four beers in that place.

"You'd break the camera," he said, raising the bottle to her.

She sailed a beer-coaster at him. "You watch what you say, mister. I own this place now."

"How'd that happen?" Tom asked.

"My husband, God rest his soul, died since the last time you were in here with your nickels and pennies."

He eyed her, wondering if they were still bantering or if he'd stuck his foot in it. "Who'd marry *you*?" he asked. "You never said anything about a husband before."

"He'd never done nothing for me before!" she said, and her face seemed to widen as she burst out in a harridan's laugh. "You're lucky I'm not sentimental, mister, or I'd have one of my boyfriends take you out back for sneering at a widow." She gestured into the room, and Tom looked back at the four or five older men hunched over their soups. He turned to the lady.

"You could be rich before you know it—" he said, "play your cards right."

★

Lillian's house was off one of the two main streets, a little side road that ran down beside the town's old grey and white cemetery. The house was a bungalow with an upper dormer and a small basement that Lillian had been renting out since she came to town to be closer to her mother. The previous year, Mrs. Brant had moved out of her independent-living apartment and into the county home. She now shared a room with an Alzheimer's case, and was miserably unhappy. It seemed Mount Morris was a place neither for a young woman nor an old one, and although she didn't say it, Lillian was waiting for her mother to die. There was no work in the town, and only the renter and a little inheritance from her father provided Lillian with enough income to pay her mortgage and buy what she needed. It was no wonder Tom had left the town the last few years feeling low. Last year he'd even "lent" Lillian money to see her through part of the fall.

She came to the door to greet him in a pair of frayed jean-shorts and a black spandex one-piece. She looked like she'd just been to a beach.

"Mistuh Lumsden," she said, squeezing him. The bodysuit made her as slick and cool as a seal. She pushed back and kissed him on both cheeks.

"You look great, Lillian." He held her waist and looked at her. Something in Lillian's genes kept her young, although he could see in her face that she was living out a hard time. She led him into the house, her little finger curled in his. It was exciting to be touched by his ex-wife. She'd always been a very physical person, at ease in her body, and he'd cherished how well the two of them had been suited as lovers. That it wasn't only uncut lust that linked them spoke to the fact that they'd been personally compatible too. It was a good and rare thing they'd had, ruined only by the fact that some of their plans hadn't matched.

The house was the same, only tidier.

"I cleaned up for you," she said.

"You didn't have to do that."

"You should have seen it, though. It looked like a bordello in here." She smiled brilliantly at him, happy to be together. "Drink, eat, or fuck?"

"God, Lillian," he said.

"We'll start at the top and go from there."

She left him in the living room and collected drink things in the kitchen. He looked around, not surprised to see the increase in knickknacks, especially the angels Lillian had been collecting since Elmira. This infantile attachment still bothered him, but he'd braced himself for it, and she knew better than to indulge herself in any reference to good spirits. She'd tried all kinds of remedies for what she thought was wrong with her life, and like a lot of people, she settled on finding some kind of faith. She'd gone from sects of her native religion (a branch of Christianity he'd never paid much attention to), to meditation religions, to group-therapy religions. But she'd come to believe in angels, really believe in them—she knew the difference between cherubim and seraphim—and for some time their likenesses had been filling the empty spots on various surfaces. Alarmingly peaceful angels adorned many of the walls and shelves in her house. Some with trumpets, many with little harmless penises. All in mid-flight. She had books on them, and, as she'd told him once, her home page was the main page of the American Ring of Angels. To his way of thinking, it was like praying to Jiminy Cricket.

She brought him a neat rye and clinked her Cinzano to it and they both drank. He told her about his day, about the little kids in the two schools getting older, how some of them remembered him from previous years, how it was like having five thousand kids of his own. She nodded at that, appearing impressed at something. He could have come any day of the year and told her that story—any day would have been like this. So it didn't feel the least bit false to tell it.

"Do you make them smile?"

"If I have to, I lick a quarter and stick it to my forehead."

She opened her mouth in awe and searched in a pocket. "Show me," she said, and held out a quarter to him. He grinned at it, but she licked it herself and then pushed a forelock of his hair up and pressed it to his skin. It stayed in place, and she clapped her hands, delighted.

"I'm a panic, aren't I?" he said.

"You're all that and a bag of chips."

He sat in the kitchen, watching her buzz around, switching her hips at him and taking the lids off pots. The place smelled terrific—the rosemary-bright scent of a roast drifted up out of the oven, and he imagined there would be little new potatoes in there too, cooking in the salty fat, and probably squash or green beans on the stove. He ate out twice a day almost every day of his life and accumulated enough leftovers during the week that he had food on the weekends (he kept a bachelor apartment about midway between all his accounts—a tiny place on the outskirts of Harrisburg), so a home-cooked meal, especially one made by Lillian, was a rare and welcome thing.

She cast little glances back at him, enjoying him being there in her home, and went into the fridge to grab a shrimp ring she'd defrosted. "You're spoiling me," he said, reaching for one. He popped it into his mouth, snapping the tail out and looking in to see if there was any meat left, then took another. She'd put an apron on, and when she passed behind him, he reached out and tugged on the knot so it came undone. She slapped at him. "Go sit somewhere else until I call you," she said.

He went and sat down on a doily-covered chair in the adjoining room. This was the main angel chamber. Half a dozen of them stood on the mantelpiece in various poses, and there was much archery. One had a clock in his belly that made Tom think of the see-through cow his dad had taken them to look at when he and his sister were little. They'd somehow taken off a patch of a cow's skin and replaced it with a window, so you could see inside. They'd stood there and watched it eat and watched the stomachs clench and release. How horrible it was, how shiny and white and horrible. The cow could even move: it wasn't glass in its body, it was like the flexible plastic his dad put on the windows in the winter and sealed with a hair dryer.

There were a few paintings of angels and one big stone one in the corner of the room, holding up a birdbath. You could fill it with water and keep the window open, he thought, and then anything with wings could fly in and wet its whistle. Angels and chickadees splashing about. He'd always had dismissive thoughts about Lillian's beliefs, and it sometimes made him feel that he didn't have enough heart to love a person the right way. But he believed you had to be willing to look at the hardest things in life and admit they were beyond your understanding. You had to submit and you had to accept you were powerless. Most people couldn't do this (probably he was one of them). And yet, to put down something as harmless as believing in angels. Wasn't it true that most people took a long time to find something to put their faith in? Lillian's beliefs had only tacked off in a direction that was strange *to him*. But as she'd said more than once, he didn't *know* strange. She knew people who slept with their gurus or went and lived in places where they told you when to eat and drink and when to go to the bathroom. She'd only ever meditated and talked about her feelings, and now she wanted to believe that there were helpful spirits looking out for her. What the hell could be wrong with that?

"Go on," she said, spying him from the kitchen. "It's

been half an hour since you came in here and so far not a word about them. You must be fit to bust."

"They're innocent-looking."

"They're 'stupid' and 'juvenile.'"

"That too. But it's not like you're standing on a street corner selling pencils for Jesus."

"At least I'm not doing that." She shook her head at him. "I've moved on from the angels, you'll be happy to know."

"Yeah?"

"I just collect them now because I like them."

He ranged back toward the kitchen. "Last time I saw you, you still took them pretty seriously. I hope I didn't say anything too nasty."

"It wasn't you," she said. "You probably think I was so horrified at your reaction that I was shaken out of my silly spiritual quest."

"No."

"I stopped because I got what I needed out of them." She looked in a pot and tucked a lock of hair back when it fell forward, then turned the heat down. "Since you last saw me, and partook of my cuisine, and then left at midnight because you had to take pictures of some backwater children the next morning, I've been up to all kinds of things."

"I'm glad to hear it," he said, tipping his drink back and bracing himself. She'd often told him that his interest in the lives of others didn't come naturally enough, and this sudden volunteering of personal news signalled to him that he'd waited too long to ask her how she was. "So it's been a busy year?"

"Oh yeah," she said. "I've been living in this house, and doing a little painting, and giving daycare from time to time for pin money. I've got some government money and some savings, so I'm not struggling too hard. I got my mom—"

"How *is* your mom?"

"You can go downstairs and ask her yourself."

He stared at her a moment, expecting her to laugh, but she didn't. He looked toward the door he knew led down there.

"She's fine," said Lillian.

"What happened to your tenant?"

"She turned into my mother. Someone must have cast a spell."

"I just thought you needed the income. Didn't you get a deal at the home?"

"They took whatever she got every month and didn't leave her a penny for anything."

He pushed some ice down into his glass. He wasn't Mrs. Brant's favorite, and he'd been the object of a letter-writing campaign for a number of months after he and Lillian split. At the beginning the letters were rational and friendly, warm even, drawing on the fullness of her experience as a long-married woman and observing that the trials of a life with someone made for hard work. She understood that he needed time apart, she knew men had to cross over something to make it to the place most women got to easily. But after he stopped replying to her letters (politely acknowledging her point of view, lightly reaffirming his own), they became surprisingly abusive. In her last letter she'd accused him of taking Lillian's best years and not having enough sense to know that he'd never do better. This last seemed more a slight against Lillian than him, but still he didn't respond. He hadn't seen Mrs. Brant since before the breakup. "Does she know I'm here?" he asked.

"She knows I'm having dinner with a friend."

"Does she know it's me?"

"I don't want to put her back in hospital, Tom. She knows it's someone I see once in a while, and if she has her suspicions, she keeps them to herself. She likes to think I'm a sensible girl."

"How can you be a sensible girl, Lillian? You got rid of your tenant and took your mother out of the only place that could take care of her."

"I take care of her fine." Her mouth had turned down hard at the suggestion that she'd endangered her own mother. "I'm not the one who finds looking after another person an unbearable load."

"Now, now," he said, and he reached out to touch her, but she pulled her hand away.

"Your only job here is to be nice."

"I'm sorry," he said. "You're a very good daughter. You are. I'd be lucky to have you."

"Fuck off, Tom."

"I'm serious." She stared at him, shaking her head a

little. "At centre, you're a much better person than I could ever have been."

She turned off all the burners. It suddenly felt that things were going to get ugly, maybe even that he'd be invited to leave. But she turned back to him, smiling pleasantly. "Do you want to eat?"

"Do you still want to feed me?"

She passed him plates down from the shelf and he went into the other room, grateful to have a job to do. They wouldn't have stayed together, he thought. There was nowhere to go with the notion. He moved around the table, turning his back to the basement door. "Does she ever mention me? Your mom?"

Lillian came through from the kitchen with a casserole dish in her hands. "Well . . . sometimes, after I've had a date that went particularly bad, she says, 'Men are useless.'"

Over dinner, he managed to muscle the mood back around to something more friendly. He knew he was too stupid to keep out of the territory they seemed to trip into in recent years, where he ended up feeling like a bastard and she became quiet or even sour. He told her his stories, the ones he thought good to tell, where he was the dopey, faintly loveable person he thought she preferred, and he complimented her on the fantastic cooking. But when the desire to seem like a kinder person was sated, all he could think about was Lillian and her mother going down the drain. It gave him a curiously numb feeling to think that someone he'd loved could end up like this. If Mrs. Brant got any government money it bought a few cartons of milk and a tank of gas a week, that was it, he was sure. The mortgage was probably coming out of whatever savings there still were from the store, maybe a little something from whatever her mother got from her dad's pension. He wished he were somewhere back in time with Lillian, right before the bad stuff started, wished he could turn back the pages of her biography to where everything still seemed possible.

He could give her a good lot of cash, but that wouldn't last. You could die in a corner in a small town like this, with no work and no one to buy your house if you needed to get out. Whoever Lillian had bought this place from had no doubt left town riding a delirious drunk: who knows how long it had been on the market. Wherever he worked, he saw two things: flags and For Sale signs. You'd be better off living on a uranium dump and collecting on the class-action suit than being a proud home owner in all the towns he knew.

"Why don't you guys rent a place somewhere and rent *this* place out?"

"Who's going to rent my whole house, Tom?"

"You got a tenant before, you could get a married couple or even a family now. They pay the mortgage and the cost of whatever place you rent."

"Say I rent somewhere with Mom, and then I can't get anyone in here. Or worse, they fuck off without paying and bash up the place?" She was waving a green bean on the end of her fork. "It's better we at least stay somewhere where we know what we owe every month."

"You're right," he said. "It's just a patch of bad luck."

"I'm not complaining Tom. I'm fine." She folded the bean into her mouth and chewed slowly, looking at him. "You're worried about me. That's nice."

"Well, I am."

"Thank you."

They ate for a while in silence. The light outside started to fade. In the forest behind Lillian's house, the early evening summer light was cutting through the trees, picking out the white skins of the birches, and here and there, thin cedars with bare branches made ribs of light in the air. What kind of effort might be going on for his benefit right now, to keep up appearances, he wondered. And yet, maybe everything would correct itself in the passing of time and Lillian would be okay. *Just a patch.* She collected the dinner things and went into the kitchen, humming as she stacked the dirty plates, then came out with two bowls of strawberry cobbler with ice cream on top and coffees she'd put whipped cream into.

"You remember all my favourites."

"I was paying attention." She sat down and ate the berries out of her bowl with her fingers. "So. Do I have the pleasure of your company tonight?"

"Yes," he said, but he kept his eyes down.

With his reassurance that she would not be alone in the night, she brightened, and they went to the couch and shared a bottle of white wine she'd saved. She bought it because it was a dessert wine, this was what the man in the spirits store had told her, and they drank much of the bottle, trying to find the right way to describe the taste. Liquory peaches, perhaps, or sugar cane in cough syrup. She stretched out along the back of the couch and regaled him with tales of her colourfully failed dates and made him laugh at small-town stupidity. She'd made Mount Morris a tolerable home, even if, in his dire imaginings it was the site of her decline. He had the disturbing, but drunken, thought that he could go into the basement when Lillian was asleep and somehow bring about her mother's death. He thought about it while she was talking and he was saying "God, really?" and "right, right," but he was trying to think of how you would go about such a thing, kill a person. He imagined he could cover her face with a pillow, but remembered that they could figure out it was a murder by the buildup of chemicals somewhere in her body. These were idle thoughts, but garishly compelling. There were probably a dozen solutions to his ex-wife's troubles.

Then, as if she were reading his mind at some angle, she said, "I've always thought it would be very humiliating to be dead. I've been to many open-casket funerals, and there's everyone looking at the body and saying what a good person he was, or how good she looks. I just can't stop thinking what a terrible thing it would be to have to be dead in front of other people."

"I understand that most people don't mind."

"I think it's worse than being nude in front of strangers. There you are, in this terribly private moment in your life, and everyone is staring at you." She paused, lengthily, and he wondered if she was thinking of one of those afternoons in a funeral parlour. He'd been in a couple with her, trying not to look at the powdery form lying inert in the box. "People touching you, even," she said at last.

He leaned forward to refill his glass. She was drunk too, and morbidly philosophical. This was how it went most years with her now: dinner, then too much wine and her mind ticking over into bleak ruminations. Loneliness, infirmity, death. It made him feel like he was back in university, sitting in a circle of people talking about the kinds of things that made people nod a lot and act like they were putting it all together for the first time.

"You must think being born is even more humiliating then," he said. "There you are, in a compromising position, naked and all."

"I hadn't thought of it," she said.

"It's a good thing most people are only minors when it happens, or there'd be some arrests. 'Well, Mrs. Smith, this is how we found'm, both feet up your wazoo. We're going to take him away for questioning. Officer Jones, swaddle'm.'"

She was looking at him over the rim of her glass. "Are you done? All I was saying is I don't want anyone staring at me after I'm gone."

"Okay."

That seemed the end of the topic for the time being, and he was glad of it. What the hell was she doing thinking about caskets anyway? He leaned over to pick up her glass, but she misread his body language and lifted her face to him and closed her eyes. He kissed her on the cheek. She opened her eyes. "You going to pat me on the head too?"

"It's late."

She pushed herself up against the back of the couch, and when she stood she had to close her eyes to let the blackness fizz up and disperse. "Geeziz," she said. "Well, let's go up then." She held out her hand to him. "C'mon, cowboy." He took her hand and pulled it toward his mouth and kissed it. Then gave it back to her.

"Maybe I should sleep on the couch here."

"Me in the bed and you on the couch? I don't remember it being quite that big."

"Well, no, it isn't."

She stood staring at him, then narrowed her eyes at him and gave him a tiny smile. "You think I'm pathetic."

"I don't—"

"You think I'm too pathetic to fuck. Is that it?"

"No, Lillian, you're not pathetic in the least."

"Look at me, okay?" She stood square to him, legs apart and fists on her hips. "I'm the most beautiful woman in Mount Morris. You'd have to go *all* the way to Hornell to find a better-looking woman than me."

"Maybe all the way to Elmira."

"I used to be the most beautiful woman in Elmira,

too." She stood in front of him, watching him not move, and she protectively brought the hand he had kissed over her stomach. "So what's the problem, then?"

"I just think I should stay down here."

She nodded, fuzzy, trying to figure him out. "So *I* should stay down *here*?"

"I don't think you should, Lillian."

Now her smile faded. "You here, me there. That's what you mean?"

"I think so. Listen Lillian, I should have—"

Before he'd finished, she was halfway up the stairs, muttering, instantly sober. He heard a closet door open, and then a shower of bedthings rained down over the banister. They came waving down like furled parachutes, and then her face appeared over the railing. She looked flushed, her face glowing a little, like there was a faint light behind her skin. "I don't beg for sex, Tom!"

"I didn't mean you—"

"I get laid *a lot!* Any time I want!"

"I know you do, Lillian."

"So I'm a slut now?"

"Let's . . ." He put his hand over his forehead.

"What."

"We're both drunk."

"So now you draw the line at drunken sluts, huh? You've raised the bar for Tom Lumsden. That's good, you got some class!"

"Now you're the one not being nice."

"Nothing's nice. Go then," she said, throwing a hand

into the air. "Some of tomorrow's best minds are probably waiting to be photographed by you, a man of good taste."

He got up to mount the stairs, but she vanished immediately and slammed her bedroom door. He stood at the bottom, collecting his breath, and then he went and pulled the sheets off the floor and the furniture and set them up on the couch. He sat for a while, staring out into the room. It had always seemed a little charmed to him, this thing they had, but now they were finally in the place most divorced couples got to before they split up. Nothing he did now would be right, and that was probably as it should be. But it made him aware, for the first time, that the place they'd been headed after their breakup had always been inevitable, and now they were there, and it made him sorrowful to realize it.

He tried to turn his mind to what his day was supposed to be like tomorrow, taking some refuge in his own order. But it was as difficult as keeping his eyes focused. He would have to find some way to give her money—this he'd already decided—but now it was going to be harder. His sample case was still in the car—he'd gone through it before lunch, looking at the orders that had come in from Wilkes-Barre and Stroudsburg. A total of seven schools, and the replies had been good. Since he came by and picked up the envelopes himself (a courtesy that encouraged people to fill out their orders), many folks paid in cash, and there was probably $800 out there. He could send her more later. He wanted to sneak downstairs and visit Mrs. Brant, if only to take an account of what kind of shape she was really in. How much more care would this person need? If he knew that, he'd know a lot. He reached for his glass and rolled the wine around in it, then tilted the remains into his mouth. Crass science, this, making money in order to live. It had killed his father, counting out his days in short piles. No up-side in retail, he'd say. Better off betting on the ponies. Retail had killed him, owing seventy cents on the dollar to the supplier, then another twenty-five on rent and payroll. Who can live off five cents? It was a good business, his father would say to him, until the big stores came in. Those guys can hold their breath until you drown.

Tom lay down and turned his back to the cool fabric along the couch's frame. Tomorrow he'd be going up above the border, to a couple of new schools in Hamilton and St. Catharines, small cities in a part of Ontario they called the Golden Horseshoe, which struck him as the kind of name a place gets called, rather than one it calls itself, like the way they called Wisconsin the Milk Jug of America, or something like that.

He settled himself, tucking the sheets between his knees, and he adjusted the pillow. He could hear the sprinklers on peoples' lawns kicking in, a series of syncopated, repeating sounds, like little races going on all around Lillian's house. He'd grown up in the suburbs of Buffalo, back in the sixties before it had become a joke and they had to spend a lot of money making it sound like everyone was actually really proud of it. But he'd had a lawn as a kid, and the same neighbours throughout his whole childhood, and bike trails only he and his friends knew. Back when his father had been proud to have a little hardware store, the family name LUMSDEN'S arced in gold paint across the front window. Later his father scraped the name off and the store was called just HARDWARE, as if it were the archetype of such a place, and little curls of gold flake drifted around the wooden floors for years after that. It was a safe, circumscribed world. Most of what he knew of all of these places was gone now. That world was still there in its way, but as part of a swelling mass that had chewed up all the neighbourhoods and little corners that had seemed so distinct to him as a child, and then as a young man.

His father had died of a heart attack. He'd been opening boxes of bird feed. An insignificant, unscheduled death while alone in the store. For years after, the theme of his father's death was all that his mother could talk about. The punishment of a good man. "And what does he get for all that?" she'd keen, and Tom would comfort her with cooing sounds and remembrances, but nothing could convince his mother that she wasn't widow to a universal injustice.

He'd used his father's death to combat Lillian's desire for children, saying he didn't want to sacrifice himself like that. But even without kids, he saw that, like his father, he was himself little more than the groove he was making in the earth. He'd just covered more territory. There was no getting away from the way life spent you, whether you were busy with children or with loneliness.

He hadn't heard her come down the stairs, and he startled when he saw her, standing at the foot of the couch, her arms crossed over her T-shirt.

"Lillian?"

"I'm sorry," she said. "It's just that I look forward to seeing you."

He pushed himself up on his elbows. "Look, I have someone," he said. "I have someone in my life now. I wanted to say something earlier—"

"I don't care." She put her knee up on the arm of couch and came toward him. "Skootch over."

He pulled the sheet away from his back and shifted to the edge of the couch, and she tucked herself into the warm space he'd left. She seemed much smaller to him now, as if he could curl up his arm and hold her against his chest like a child. She settled in on her back and reached for his arm and draped it over her belly, then closed her eyes. She smelled of soap. After a couple of minutes, he thought she was going to drift off to sleep, but then she stirred and looked at him.

"Will you take a picture of me?" she said. "You probably don't have any pictures of me like I am now."

"Yes," he said. "Let's do that. We'll do it in the morning."

"No, let's do it now. I want you to have a picture of me from right now."

He shrugged and pulled the sheet back. He was so tired that in the near-dark he saw a pale strobing in front of his eyes. He had a 35-mm with a fast film in it in the glove compartment of his car; he could take her in the light from the kitchen. He went out front in his bare feet, where the suffused glow he'd seen from inside resolved into the sharpness of streetlamps. There were clouds in front of the moon, and a fog obscured the top of the road where he'd turned off the main street and come down past the cemetery earlier in the day. He got the camera out of his glove compartment and went into the trunk to get the money from the cigar box where he kept it. He put the eight hundred into his pocket and went back in.

Lillian was sitting up in the middle of the couch, her legs tucked under her bottom, her hair twisted down over one shoulder. She looked perfect to him then, as she'd always done when he caught her in an unguarded moment. He switched on the light in the kitchen, then approached her and turned her a little toward him.

"Don't pose me," she said. "Just like this." She sat straight again, and one side of her face fell into darkness.

He brought the camera up to his eye. "You want me to have half a picture of you?"

"You can come back for the other half if it's not enough."

He shot a frame and advanced the film, but she got up. "Just one." She went toward the door to the basement. "Take one of me with my mother as well."

"Come on, Lillian."

She stood at the door and put her hand on the knob. Then smiled and backed away. Where she was, the light from the kitchen had flipped her to shadow. It picked up the texture of the skin on her legs and made the edges of her hair glow in a corona of blue-black light. He wanted to take another picture, and he reached for the camera. This could be the other half, he thought, this shape in front of me. But she saw him pick up the camera and said, "Don't." He let it back down.

"I'm sorry, Lillian," he said.

She folded her arms over her chest. "I guess that's our night."

"I guess it is."

"You know, I don't usually sleep alone. Did I tell you that?" She lifted her eyes into the light. "I go downstairs, or she comes up here. I told her she should just stay up here with me, but she thinks it's important that I live like an independent person. Funny, huh?"

He was looking up toward her and squinting a little. His eyes hurt. "What part?"

"That she thinks if I'm alone up here I'm independent."

"Maybe she's just respecting your privacy."

"I like sleeping with her. Does that sound odd? It's like this is my last chance to have her to myself, just the way I wanted when I was a kid. I cook for her and make her all the things she used to make me, and at night we talk in bed. She tells me stories about myself when I was a little girl. Apparently, I was a *fanciful* child."

"See? You're not alone at all. I don't even have that."

"She sleeps with her back against my chest and I can feel her ribs go up and down against the inside of my arm, and I listen to her breathing."

"That's nice. Really, it is."

"That's something we could have done for each other, Tom. But I guess that didn't happen."

"No." He thought of the money in his pocket.

"Did you ever cheat on me?"

"Why ask me that now?"

"One of the men in the bank liked me," she said. "He even told me."

"But you didn't."

"I should have," she said. "But my optimism made me stupid."

He turned his mouth toward his shoulder and coughed a little and then smiled at her, to show he wasn't hurt, but he was surprised how much the comment stung him. It had never occurred to him that their breakup was anything more than the result of cross-purposes. He'd never seen it as a failure of hope. "I want you to know," he said, "that I've always come to see you because I *wanted* to. Not because I thought I should."

She laughed her high, abrupt laugh and came over to where he was sitting. She leaned down to kiss him and her hair fell over his face as she touched her mouth to his. She said his name. Then she straightened and gestured to the couch. "That thing pulls out, you know. You don't have to sleep on it like you're too drunk to go home." She pushed a chair back in under the table, passing it on her way back to the basement door. "You don't come to see me out of guilt, Tom. I know that."

"I don't."

"You do it because you still care about me, and that's much worse."

When she went downstairs, he took the cushions off the couch, and stared at the skeletal frame. It would be six hours to Toronto, and he couldn't drive it now. It shook him to realize how much he wanted to see Linda. This kind of attachment, that brought with it the foreignness of longing, had never been in his life before. He moved the camera to a sidetable, its weight in his hand a familiar gravity. Inside it, the last last picture of Lillian lay there like a leaf inside a stone. He'd told her everything he thought he could, although he'd come ready to tell her more. But it turned out he hadn't had the heart to tell her the rest. He hadn't, until very recently, he realized, had the heart for much, and the cost of that had been another person's happiness.

LONG DIVISION

"No natural notion of infinity is compatible
with the laws of arithmetic."
—TIMOTHY GOWERS, *MATHEMATICS, A VERY SHORT
INTRODUCTION*

Catherine Nilson waited outside of Room 23, beside the
mural of Canadian Sports Heroes, on the second floor of
Harrison Road Public School. This was where her only
child, an eight-year-old son, attended his advanced classes,
and where she meant to intercept him before he went into
math, a subject taught by a round man about her age
named Mr. Melvin. He'd noted her idling outside his
classroom at five minutes to one, just as lunch was ending.
He'd never met her before (her husband, Andy, had come
to meetings at the school, averring that he was the parent
more involved in Daniel's education), and so he passed
her a curious look, but said nothing before entering his
class.

All around her, the post-lunch crowd was reassembling
beside the double-row of lockers. The looks of the third
and fourth graders unnerved Catherine. It had been
almost thirty years since she'd been subject to the laws of
that society, and the way these small men and women
registered her presence made her think of her own early

education, in which she'd run the gamut of cat-eyed
eight-year-olds with their withering murmurs and their
scorekeeping. In the short time she'd been waiting, she'd
become aware that she was the only subject of conversation in the second-floor hallway. There was no
whispering or pointing, however: the subculture of
prepubescent children was like heart cells in a Petri dish.
Connected by a matrix of unseen fibres, they tended to
beat in unison.

Daniel's classmates began arriving, but he was not
among them yet. It troubled her to see what they had
traded up for when Daniel had been put into this
accelerated group. These too-intelligent kids, already cut
free from the moorings of what was popular, had the look
about them of an underclass. Their rucksacks lacked logos,
their clothing and haircuts were plain. They shuffled into
Mr. Melvin's classroom to have this advanced math
pounded into them, and in this fashion they were just so
much clay, no different than the rest of their schoolmates.
But the rest of their schoolmates had been deemed *average*,
so they got to have fun and trade hockey cards and get co-
opted by soft drink companies and running shoe brands.
Daniel's friends were to be moulded by *higher learning*, but
molded no less. She'd had this disagreement, complete
with her own italics, many times with Andy, and he'd
always trumped her with what he called her pretensions to
commonness. They had a special child, he'd say, and she
seemed ashamed of that. She would throw in the towel at
this point, because going any further would mean trying

to explain that she was not ashamed of Daniel, but rather she wished she could see more of herself in him. A little of *her* commonness, she thought, could see him through a great deal of trouble.

So here she was, having taken the afternoon off from her firm, on this Wednesday in the late fall, to try to pull Daniel down a little from the ether of his education and back into the oxygen of normality. She was here with her husband's blessing, having convinced him that the corrective she intended to deliver was essential to the boy's growth. She was here to make Daniel own up to a lie. The fact that she had caught him in it was pure luck, but it had enlivened her hopes that he was not so unique that he did not need to conceal a weakness, occasionally. She longed for him to *have* weaknesses, to try something and fail. It was a strange way to express her love, to want him to taste the poison of disappointment. She thought if he did, though, he might develop its antibodies: humility, humour, resilience.

As she waited outside Mr. Melvin's room Catherine kept her gaze away from the students, uncomfortable with their eyes on her. It was as if they already knew she was here to betray one of their own.

It had taken to grade three before Daniel's teachers figured out what she and Andy already knew. His mental capacity did not indicate a talent for mere retention; he *synthesized*. That was the educational word for it. It meant that *given A and B*, Daniel could *therefore C*. This was not as simple an ability as recognizing that fire and paper were things that became smoke and ash. Daniel's mind could work deductively too, tracing back from ash to smoke to paper and then to an unlit match.

Catherine never thought of herself as particularly intelligent, although no one would have called her slow. She had never much valued the more abstract arts of mind. *A head for numbers* was the kind of thing people back where she was from would have said euphemistically, meaning a person was useless for outdoor work, or was dreamy. But it wasn't as if she'd grown up without books or math. Just that it was deemed somewhat perverse to focus on either, and so it had always seemed very odd to her to have ended up with a child who did.

At first, she would have said Daniel was unlike Andy too. When they'd first met, twelve years earlier, they were a young couple finishing off their masters degrees at the University of Toronto, she in psychology, he in social work. They met on a rainy night, at a party in an apartment overlooking Bathurst; Andy had opened the door and passed Catherine a glass of red wine, as if he'd decided he was going to seduce the next person who came in. Everyone was crammed into the kitchen, and the two of them spent the next three hours face to face, draining bottles of wine he kept setting aside for their personal use. When the party thinned out, they went and faced each other, leaning against a wall in what some nineteenth-century family would have properly used as a dining room, but that was now crowded with LP-filled milk crates and bookshelves made out of bricks and wooden planks.

"What do you think you're doing?" she said, looking back and forth between his eyes and his mouth. He'd touched her long black hair, hair he didn't yet know made her look like her mother when she'd been Catherine's age, jet-black Nana Mouskouri hair. Catherine usually kept it tied up in a scrunchy that came loose once or twice an hour, allowing her to sweep it forward and tidy it back into the plush elastic. "You think you're going to kiss me?"

"I'm drunk. I'm trying my luck."

She put a hand on his chest and pushed him away. "I'm a game of skill," she said. His jaw slackened in erotic paralysis, but she kept her face still, determined not to show him that she was also having trouble mastering herself. Just an hour earlier, she hadn't even known that this man existed. And now she was tipping forward into a future—however limited it may turn out to be—with him.

(Sometimes, Catherine imagines that she's gone back to this same moment, knowing what she knows now. But she doesn't know if she would tell herself what awaited them. What kind of life would have ensued if she had leaned into him and said, *We will have a strange child and never quite know how to feel about him, and it will make it hard to love each other?*)

"You're beautiful," he said, and she turned her back to the wall and let him carry on. She could feel a strange mound against her lower spine. "When you came through the door," he said, "I thought I'd punch anyone who tried to talk to you. Even a girl."

"How hard?"

"*Really* hard," he said, and she laughed and crooked her forefinger into the top of his pants and pulled him to her. She had one hand on the back of his neck and she could feel the muscles there straining as she pushed her mouth against his. He tasted like sour blackberries. She'd figured out the bump against her lower back was a patch of Polyfilla the size of a platter; she relaxed against it, taking more of the pressure from Andy's body until finally she felt the wall give way, and the huge bolus of plaster went clattering down to the basement inside the walls.

She was going to be a passionate woman. She was figuring this out.

They never married. They were joined by flesh, as Andy sometimes put it, the body of their son a bridge between them. She stood with Andy over the crib, looking down, the baby's lips moving thickly over an invisible nipple, the nub of his tongue pulsating at the opening. Some days she would think *is this my life?* and other days, *this is my life.* Fear and awe in a cycle. She loved Daniel. She'd bury her mouth in his hot neck and suck and he'd squirm in delight. And those legs—like pizza dough sold in bulging plastic bags, dimpled dough legs so fat they rippled when he laughed. It's so easy to love a baby.

Then his abilities appeared. They looked in the books for the stages he was supposed to be going through, but he didn't go through them the way the books promised. He was supposed to like faces, but he didn't like them as much as he seemed to *examine* them. Held up, Daniel would stare at some facial feature: an eye, or the whorl of an ear. Before he was one, he'd touch his mother's nose and then his own. When he was supposed to be sucking on his toys and hurling them to the floor, he instead used them as tools. The chunky plastic blocks other children would stack into saliva-glazed towers, he'd use to make straight lines across the living room floor, neatly bisecting it into triangles or rectangles. They watched him as if he were something that had crashed through their skylight one evening. An alien houseplant, an unknown species. Andy got used to it though. His experience allowed him to accommodate a strange new mind. This is what Catherine told herself: her *lack* of experience meant that what seemed marvellous to Andy would, for some time, seem abnormal to her. It was a matter of catching up.

Daniel muddled through the boredom of early school, but his pent-up intelligence burst its confines in Grade 3, and in early September of that year, he'd stood up in Mrs. Renald's class and declaimed passionately on the beauty and mystery of math. This had come just as his homeroom was to tackle double-digit addition, and Mrs. Renald had written *14+37=* on the blackboard. She was going to demonstrate the power of vertical formulation, but the vision of the numbers with their operators had caused Daniel's fervour to coalesce.

"The equals sign is like a magic trick," he'd said, standing and speaking as if he were merely a conduit for a voice from another place. "Before it, numbers gather and decide to do things together. Fourteen, thirty-seven . . . they want to be something else. This is why they come. Sometimes they join together, or one takes itself away, like it's digging a hole in the other number. Or one number will come together with another number as many times as that other number is. Or it will take itself out of that number as many times as it can, until there's nothing left. That's called division." He'd been gesturing with his hands about the room, as if the figures he was speaking of had taken form in the air around him. Then he lowered his eyes again to his bewildered classmates. "But this isn't the best thing about numbers," he said. "What's really neat is that *everything* is math. Like, if you add time and pressure to coal, that equals diamonds." (He'd considered going to the front of the room and taking up some chalk to write $C + (TxP) = D$, but he did not want to confuse them.) "Or this:" he continued. "Water, divided by heat, equals steam. The whole world is like this."

Mrs. Renald had smiled and nodded, and some of his classmates were staring at him in juvenile revulsion. Perhaps they were going to have to learn this, too?

It was not his fault that the connections between things filled his mind: he could see the webbing under the skin of the world. The next day, after the visit to the principal, he was placed in another class.

Long before this moment, Andy had decided to feed this wondrous little brain. He glued pictures of animals and vehicles and vegetables to the ceiling above the crib. He lay on the floor with a long pointer and touched the objects, saying their names, so that Catherine imagined her son's dreams were like a murmuring dictionary: *tractor, platypus, treefrog, eggplant*—all these words that Daniel was too young to understand. She worried his mind was being dragged away from the dreams of colour and faces and sounds she thought all infants needed. But Andy insisted they had to give this bright infant *information*. He was a bigger sponge than most babies. Catherine had to admit that in Red Deer they didn't see very much of this, and if they had, maybe they wouldn't have known what to do. It was entirely possible that Andy's approach was the right one.

Just the same, she was worried to see hints of a certain part of Andy become fully blown tendencies now. He'd always been neat, but now he feared germs. He smelled his food before he ate it. He could not sit and have a simple conversation unless he was also somehow marshalling what he perceived to be the burgeoning chaos around them. He would eat dinner while poring over bank statements, colour-coding debits according to *household, automotive, food*, and so on, and checking off the amounts against cheque stubs or receipts or ATM slips. Catherine tried to think of this behaviour in a humorous light—a friend had once called it *non-benign thoroughness*—but she worried that he was sucking Daniel into its vortex. She'd sit at their table, her son at one end with his removable tabletop covered in glistening smears, her husband at the other, a napkin stuck in his shirt collar, five individual decks of Post-It notes arrayed in front of him like a child's toy. (She once fantasized about taking a cheque still attached to its stub and burning it. A cheque gone awry in a world of unconsummated commerce— how it would have driven him crazy.)

Perhaps the hardest thing to do was to accept how all of this made her feel toward Andy physically. The deeper his fascination with the baby's mind, the more he repelled her. He seemed more and more an ethereal being to her, drawn by pure rationality. She could live through anything but this. She communicated through her body. She was not a *discusser*, she was not good at it. If things got bad, she preferred to fuck. It seemed now as though a long time separated her from when she'd been someone's lover.

Over time, this state of affairs had led to fighting. The last recourse of passion. They would fight after supper, over the rushing water, when they thought Daniel could not hear them. But the sound of their voices swirled up from the kitchen, through all the noises of the house, like an electrical current in a twisted wire, directly to his ear.

When his parents fought, it was like shaking a jar with oil and vinegar in it. It would mix in a frenzy of bubbling, but as soon as you put it down somewhere, the oil would slink back up to the top, and the vinegar, as white and peaceful as a tub full of water, would settle as well. He knew his parents tried to regulate themselves, but these sudden and brief bursts of temper were the result of their caution.

Daniel believed he understood unhappiness: it was as

simple a thing as pain, which ran along nerve endings inside the body. He'd found a picture of nerves on the Internet—a red branching throughout the body that was filled with signals. Unhappiness had a web like that, except it went inside and out. All feelings worked this way, he'd come to realize. Although you could not make someone feel the heat on your palm, or a pain in your tooth, feelings travelled in longer channels. It was possible that his own unhappiness, therefore, had made his parents unhappy. He strived to be happier, but he could not. He had troubles and he had fears; happiness would come later if he was lucky. He listened to the bits and pieces of conversation that reached him in his room. Sometimes he tapped the things he heard into his computer, to see where the mysteries of his parents' marriage might be rooted.

You can't second guess every last thing returned "a high-five between people who have correctly handicapped a race together can sprain a wrist."

His mother said, *He needs to be a child, too.* That got him "in the unlikely event an intruder enters his bedroom, with the night-light on, he'll be able to see and alert you by blowing the whistle."

You could connect and reconnect in so many directions. There was no centre in the world.

School was his life, it delighted him. He brought home the disciplines of learning to his house and studied his parents with it. The scientific method said you drew conclusions by first observing nature, classifying the data you found there, conducting rational experimentation, proposing an explanation for phenomena, and then expressing your findings mathematically.

Mornings provided plenty of data; breakfast production gave coordinates that correlated to his parents' marriage. If his mother cooked, there would be hot food: eggs, waffles, sometimes porridge. If his father made breakfast, it was cold cereal. Hot food meant his mother had come downstairs before his father. His father would join them, and the three of them would eat together if it was an especially lucky morning, or at least Daniel would eat with his father, his mother having already taken her tea and toast.

However, if his father made breakfast, it meant that his mother had already left which was bad, or was still in bed, which was much worse because it meant either that she did not want to see them in the morning, or she had not slept well.

Giving each of these four possibilities a weight, Daniel classified this data on a graph:

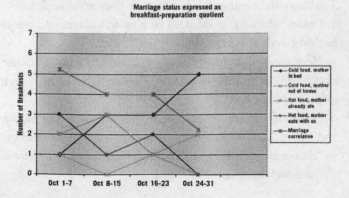

Marriage status expressed as breakfast-preparation quotient

He weighted "hot food, mother eats with us" (the most desirable condition) four times more than "cold food, mother in bed" (the least desirable) and calculated the Marriage Correlative as the weekly mean given those weights. And if the monthly average of the MC fell below 4, he considered the safety of his family life at risk.

He could see from this that things were falling apart.

One morning, a good morning, his mother was stirring eggs in the frying pan. She put a plate down in front of him and stroked his cheek with the back of her hand. His father was still shaving; Daniel could hear the frenzied buzz of the electric shaver eating the stubble off his father's cheeks.

"I want to tell you something," she said, standing on the other side of the table with the wooden spoon still in her hand. "Okay? Listen: people fight. It's okay. It's normal."

"I know. Tigers pretend-fight when they're babies. That way they can catch food when they're older."

"Mm," she said, nodding. His hair was black, and thick like dog-hair. "You should eat up."

He squeezed a thin, straight line of ketchup onto his eggs. "What's the difference between eternity and infinity?" he asked.

"Danny," she said, her voice tightening. "Your daddy and I love each other. You know that, right?"

"And you love me, and Daddy loves me."

"We *both* love you," she said.

"I know." *Hot breakfast*, he thought. His father came into the room in his suit.

"Infinity and eternity are similar concepts," he said, pulling his chair out. "They describe things that go on forever. Infinity applies to numbers, and eternity to time."

"Infinity is how much we love you," said his mother, glancing at his father, "and eternity is how long."

"Some people think zero divided by zero is infinity," said Daniel, and they looked at him. "It isn't, though."

"What is it then?" his father asked.

"It isn't anything," replied Daniel. "In math, you can't even ask the question."

It was an evening in late October when Catherine saw her glimmer of hope. She'd come up the stairs after doing the dishes alone; Andy had gone for a drive. When she clammed up the way she often did these days, he got into the car and drove off his exasperation. Daniel was on his computer; she watched him from the doorway. The screen threw a complex of light over the boy's face, it was reversed in blue squares in each of his eyes. He looked down from the screen to some paper on the desk beside him, and then back up. He tapped on his keyboard, and wrote something on the paper. He did this at regular intervals until he reached the bottom of the page. She pushed the door open and stood there. In his silence, when he presented the image of a quiet little boy with mussed hair, he took her breath away.

"Dad left," he said, still looking at his screen. "Maybe he went back to his office?"

"We had a fight. We're fighting a lot."

"I know," he said. "I can predict when you're going to fight."

"How?"

He clicked on the side of his screen, and the program changed; there was a burst of colour, lines and circles. She stepped into the room to look more closely, but as she approached the desk, he hid the program. "I can't explain it to you," he said.

"Do you think I won't understand?"

"I mean it's not finished. The model." She nodded, still smiling, but her pulse had quickened. He returned to what he was looking at when she first stopped in the hallway. She saw now that it was a calculator, but on the Internet. Below the calculator, sums and formulae scrolled up and disappeared behind it. "It's all the things people are calculating—on this page, right now, all over the world," he told her.

He'd been using it to complete his own homework. That was the paper on the desk beside him. She saw the problems were filled in neatly. "Did you do all this with the calculator?"

"Yeah," he said. "If I push my own icon here, it takes me to a page where people can give me problems to solve based on the ones I punch in. A guy from Russia gave me some."

"But you're using a calculator. How can you learn

anything that way?" He turned his eyes to her. He was frowning, but he looked tired. He always looked tired, she thought. Maybe they should move the computer into another room and limit his time. She knew what Andy would say to that. "Do you ever look at anything else on the Internet?" she asked him. "Apart from math? Do you ever, you know, look at girls?"

"Do you know when one plus one equals three?" he asked.

"No, I don't, Daniel."

"When you make a baby." He was looking at her mildly now. Why had she asked him that question? It occurred to her momentarily that she would gladly have taken his looking at naked women on the 'net over doing math with anonymous Russians. *This is how desperate I'm becoming?* "One boy and one girl make one baby and that's three. It's a joke," he said.

"A funny math joke," Catherine replied quietly. "Are you allowed to use a calculator to do your homework, Daniel?"

"Yeah . . ."

"*Are* you?" He didn't answer this time. She looked down at the paper again. The questions swarmed like Sanskrit before her eyes. This was accelerated math, but Christ, was it possible that it was too hard for him? Was he using the calculator to figure out these questions? *Was he floundering?* She asked him again, "Daniel, is it true? Your teacher told you you can use a calculator to do your *math* homework?"

He kept his face from her and replied with a breathy silence.

"Daniel, I asked you a question."

"I want you to leave now," he said.

"School is supposed to be giving you the *skills* to think things out on your own."

"Get out of my bedroom."

She leaned on his desk, so he would have to look at her. "If I ask Mr. Melvin, he's going to tell me you're allowed to use a calculator, right?"

He looked at her now, and it seemed as though the whites of his eyes were glowing. He tried to speak, but instead his mouth trembled. Catherine straightened, too surprised to comfort him. He'd lied to her! He'd calmly, wilfully, lied to her. "Go," he sobbed, and she backed out of the room. Andy was standing at the bottom of the stairs, the car keys dangling from his finger. "What's going on?" he said.

"Daniel told me a lie." She came down the stairs and passed him on her way back to the kitchen without another word.

In the morning, Daniel came down to find his father alone in the kitchen, and a bowl of corn flakes on a placemat. This brought the Marriage Correlative down to 1.8, a very bad sign. He sat quietly and poured the milk from a glass jug, and put nine blueberries on top of the corn flakes in a square. It was child's play to connect them with four lines and he didn't even bother.

He ate silently.

His father sat down across from him, the steam from his coffee rising straight up and then suddenly flattening out, left and right. Daniel stared at it, trying to figure it out.

"What are you looking at?"

"The steam," said Daniel. "It stops going straight up."

His father looked down into his coffee, and then nodded to himself. "It's the air from my nose, sweetie. It pushes the steam off to the side."

"Move your face."

His father did, and both of them watched the steam go up higher before dispersing into the cool air. It was a satisfying experiment. "Tell me something," his father said. "Did you tell your mother a lie last night?"

"No."

"Are you lying right now?"

Daniel breathed out heavily. "No."

His father laughed softly. "How about now?"

"Yes," said Daniel. "And before you ask again, this time I really lied."

"What's *I always lie*?"

"A logical fallacy," said Daniel, repeating something. "It can't be true."

"Good, hon."

He got dropped off at school and waved goodbye to his father. Most of the day, school was his haven and refuge. When he went through the doors and the bell rang, Daniel knew that the hours from the beginning to the end of the school day would be like getting on a train, and that train would go on down the track and let him off at lunch and then wait there to take him on again to three o'clock. The recesses he could handle, even though it meant being around kids who spent their time loudly comparing skills and possessions. He scared the other kids, and they didn't even make fun of him. There was something about him they didn't *get*, and that made it hard to put him down. He gave no reactions, and reactions were the stock-in-trade of the playground. So he was left to wander around and look at the school and the street, and take math out into the world with him. Sometimes he spent time with the ugly kids and the ones who played fantasy games, but mostly he stood out on the sidewalk in front of the school and made the world collapse into formulae.

Lunch was the longest break, and often Daniel would spend it in the library. If the weather was particularly good, he'd be forced out into the world of play and have to make the best of it. This October afternoon was almost warm, and Daniel went to the edge of the school grounds and looked around in the grass for coins and sat and watched the groups of kids moving from one area to another. Then the bell rang and he waited for all the other kids to go inside before he ambled in himself, careful to head up the stairs to the math room with at least thirty seconds to spare. He had synchronized his watch to the official clock in the office and knew he could take the two flights of stairs from the exterior doorway to the heavy door on the second level with about forty seconds to make it to the room before the buzzer went.

He came through the door to see the hallway empty, as he expected, but then he noticed the figure beside Mr. Melvin's classroom. It was his mother. She turned to him with a look of relief on her face, but that expression vanished and became worry. He crept up to her and the buzzer went off, signalling the beginning of the afternoon classes. Mr. Melvin went to close his door and saw the two of them standing there.

"Daniel?" he said, and looked back and forth between them. "Is there a problem, Mrs. Nilson?" Catherine suddenly felt she had no business being there, none at all. Didn't all kids cut corners in order to get on to the things they liked better? The disdain she'd sensed in the hallway before Daniel's arrival was just what she deserved. "Mrs. Nilson," his teacher repeated, "is there something wrong?"

"It's just a little problem," she said. But maybe this was the cost of doing the right thing. She could not expect to be loved and also parent this remarkable child the best way possible, and Andy had abdicated this responsibility, hadn't he?

Mr. Melvin was waiting, a look of tired expectation on his face. Disappointment was not an unusual thing in his field, she could tell, it was just a matter of what form it would take. Daniel's classmates, those in the front row, were craning their necks to see out into the hallway. Mr. Melvin shut the door. "I think we're waiting for *you*," he said to Daniel.

"No. She can tell you," he said.

Catherine straightened her back and exhaled loudly. In the little window in the door she could see a gathering of heads coming slowly into the front of the classroom. She made praying hands in front of herself and leaned toward Mr. Melvin. "Well," she said, "I felt you should know that last night I caught Daniel using a calculator to do his math homework." She waited a moment. "I thought it was something *he* should tell you, but maybe I'm partly responsible, too." She lowered her hands. Both her son and his teacher were waiting to see if she was finished, so she said, "Maybe I'm not supervising him closely enough, I mean. That's all."

Mr. Melvin nodded thoughtfully. "Thank you, Mrs. Nilson," he said. "But he *is* allowed to use his calculator. It's part of the Grade 3 curriculum." He looked down at Daniel. "He should have told you that."

Mr. Melvin opened the door and the crowd inside scattered to its places. Daniel went to his seat.

"He's very talented," said his teacher. "But I suppose he's a little forgetful about the details."

In the rear-view mirror, Catherine watched Daniel get into the back seat, dragging his plain blue knapsack behind him. She couldn't find anything to say to him, and his attention was screwed to the quiet scenes outside the window: the children waiting for their lifts, the school buses making their final on-board counts before heading off into the suburbs. She checked her mirror and, in silence, pulled out and turned left up the hill.

On the seat beside her she had his favorite take-out, roasted chicken from a franchise owned by a country singer. She'd splurged and bought all the sides: country biscuits, garlic mashed potatoes, roasted corn, even saw-mill gravy, which she despised. The scent of the dinner filled the car with a lemony, garlicky smell.

She stole little looks at him, but Daniel seemed settled, lost in his thoughts, and he made no effort to acknowledge her. She didn't remember the last time she'd seen him angry. Upset, yes, as he had been the previous night, but not angry. Was this silence anger? If so, maybe he had something in common with her after all. She could respect that. She could learn to respect that.

She'd always believed that the ones you loved had a reflection that resided in yourself, and that this kept you safe from losing track of the way they would change. And yet she knew this was not true anymore with Andy; that mirror had bent away from a real reflection some time ago, and what she had of him was not who he was. Trying to love him with the information she had was like trying to grasp something underwater without correcting for the refraction. These days, her hand was closing on nothing.

And how far off true was she with Daniel? She realized her own parents had never been aware that they'd strayed from her as the years went on, the angle of their error increasing the distance between them as time went on. To go back to the time when Andy was kissing her against that wall! What of being in her childhood hallways, gripping as if a steel bar the trajectory of her parents' lives and her own, bending it back to stay in line with the way things really were in that house?

A lost cause. She despaired of ever having the chance to change their courses. She looked up again at Daniel. "I'm so sorry," she said now. "I did a terrible thing."

He brought his eyes around to hers in the mirror and shrugged mildly. "It's okay."

"It's not okay," she said. "I broke trust with you. A parent shouldn't do that."

"I was telling you the truth."

"I know." She was coming up to their street, and she turned onto it. "You were telling the truth, and yet when I said I was going to ask Mr. Melvin, you cried. I guess that confused me."

He was looking back out the window, the connection broken once again. This was one of the immutable laws of attachment: inadmissibility. If she could know his thoughts . . . Such a thing to be wished for. It was the kind of wish a child would make, but she was someone's mother now, someone's partner, and she was alone with the ones she loved. She asked, "So then why did you cry, Daniel?" and—knowing even if he could tell her, she would not really know—asked again, "Why did you cry?"

SPLIT

The casino was on a reservation—a lot of them are now, all lit up, with valet parking and girls selling cigars. I'd crossed the border fairly groggy from the drive and sick of my CDs and I needed a break. Linda was probably asleep by now, and I'd made a little extra this trip, selling a few more portrait packages in the towns between Trumansburg and West Convex. I figured she wouldn't want me driving in the rain as tired as I was. I went in and washed my face, ran a comb through my wet hair, tried to make myself look presentable. Out on the floor, I started looking around for the five-dollar tables. One of the pit bosses told me to head upstairs where all the smoking rooms were and I might find something to my liking there.

The lowest table I found was a ten-dollar minimum, and as soon as I sat down the fat college student who was dealing warned me the minimums were going up. I told him, I only have a hundred bucks anyway, I'll be gone before then. I was surprised they weren't running any five-dollar tables. It was a Monday and the parking garage was half-empty, despite the fact that it'd been raining, and the rain usually brought people in. I guessed it was just that they had to set some standards and if you let people play for five bucks a hand then maybe the riff-raff will start coming.

The table had some quality people around it. The lady at first base chain-smoked and kept losing like she was perfecting it. There was a young couple beside her, then me, then an old Vietnamese man with stubble, and, at the end of the table, two guys who had to be regulars and played everything by the book. The guy right at third base—the last seat—had a pillar of black chips in front of him. He kept talking to the lady at first base, saying things like, "You should hit a soft seventeen against a three," and "Usually you don't double down ten against a ten." Stuff like that. Whether she played a hand the way you're supposed to, or she went with her intuition, she lost, so I don't know why Third Base was talking to her.

I knew the guy beside me was Vietnamese, because anytime you looked at him he'd nod quickly and say, "Viet Nam," and then you'd have to say, "Good," and he'd nod again and go back to his cards. I imagine he was trying to start a conversation, but no one was talking to him because he was queering the deal, hitting every hand to seventeen, regardless what the dealer had. So the two guys after him kept doing the math on his cards, figuring out what hands he was wrecking for them. It's a simple game, blackjack, you just try to beat the dealer without going over twenty-one, but for a lot of people there's more than that involved. For instance, you don't hit a total of fourteen against a dealer's two because chances are he's got a ten under and he'll bust his twelve just as quick as you'll bust your fourteen. Except he *has* to draw, and you don't. This was the very situation that was riling the guys at the end of the table.

"That would have been eighteen for me against his two, Viet Nam," said the guy between Viet Nam and Third Base, "except now you're bust hitting your fourteen to twenty-three and I have to take Jonas's card and he's got to take the dealer's. You see a two or three and you've got at least a twelve? Sit tight, okay?"

"Okay," said Viet Nam, but he'd been watching the guy talk and he only spoke when he stopped.

"He's okay, Mike," said Jonas. Jonas had a pale yellow scar right straight along the base of his throat. "Everyone's playing for pennies."

First Base laughed at that. I'd only been sitting for ten minutes, but I'd seen her lose more than two hundred dollars. The dealer dealt out the end of the shoe, then started shuffling. The young couple left, and an eyeline opened up between me and First Base.

"Your hair's wet," she said.

"See, I've got some sense."

She smiled and lit a cigarette. "I've lost fifteen hundred dollars tonight. This guy deals me a hard thirteen every chance he gets."

The dealer laughed. His name was Jimmy. I'd noticed a few dealers at the tables I'd scoped out with nametags that said Jimmy. No doubt this was some kind of cheap dealer insurance, insurance that you didn't turn around in the street when someone you'd dealt out of a few thousand dollars called "Hey, Jimmy!"

"What are you laughing at?" she said.

"You *want* to lose, Arlene. You must have some kind of inheritance or something."

"Is that any of your business, Jim?" He shook his head no. "Then shuffle the fucking cards and let's get on with this."

"If you're *looking* to lose it, you'd do better at one of the higher stake tables," I said.

"Do you crunch your hard candy, or do you suck it, mister?"

I blinked a couple times at her.

"I like mine to last," she said.

Jimmy dealt. The space between me and Arlene stayed open. Jim dealt her a hard fifteen, me two face cards, Viet Nam a twelve, Mike a blackjack (Jim had been really nice when he laid the ace, saying, "Good luck on your ace, Mike"), and he dealt Jonas a pair of threes. Jim showed a four. The play against a four is stand on anything higher than eleven. Everyone knows that.

"Hard call on those threes," said Arlene.

"Is it," said Jonas. Arlene hit and bust her fifteen. "There you go," said Jonas. "He's like a sixty-five percent chance to bust and you hit a fifteen." She smiled angelically at him.

"There're still twenty-four cards in each deck that could've made my hand, J. So shut the fuck up."

I stuck. Viet Nam took an eight to make twenty, and Mike and Jonas shook their heads.

"Let's see," said Jonas. "Arlene's ten gives me thirteen

on my first three, so I stand on that, and your eight, which you shouldn't have taken, gives me eleven on my second three, a perfect double-down against a four. But am I bitter? No. Hit me, Jim." Jim laid Jonas a nine. "Nice, a twelve," said Jonas. "Don't I feel safe. Stand," he told Jim, and Jim moved to the second three and dealt him a queen. "Twelve and thirteen," said Jonas. "Two losing hands to one, and no double to cover my ass should Jimmy here fail to bust. Go on, Jim."

Jim revealed a nine for thirteen. "Aw, this is a sure bust hand," he said. He dealt himself an ace and then a three. Then shook his head. He collected both of Jonas's bets, and paid me and Viet Nam. Viet Nam gave Jonas a thumbs up.

"You see, man?" said Jonas. "I'm glad you won. But that was your hand to lose and mine to make a little. That's just the way it goes."

"Viet Nam," said Viet Nam.

"I know." Jonas looked down at his chips. "I know, man, Viet fucking Nam. You're breaking my heart here."

We kept on playing down the shoe. Eventually a guy with a face like a whippet came and sat between me and Arlene. I would have loved to photograph that face of his—just point him at the camera and focus on the tip of his nose. It's an amazing effect you can get with these deep faces, the eyes all set back and fading.

He played progressive, which is to say he doubled his bet every time he lost. As long as you don't lose your whole bankroll, it's a sure way to double your original ten bucks every time you finally win a hand. But every progressive bettor is a cheap amateur and they all come to a point where they can't risk the hundred and sixty bucks they'll have to lay to stay the course, so they go back down to ten and kiss half their stake goodbye. The Nose was gone in fifteen minutes, right at the end of the shoe. Jonas watched him go off.

"You note how not one of us gave that shmuck a hand, hey? At least Viet Nam's playing to a strategy, no matter how it sucks. I hate fucking progressives."

Jimmy tapped the table. "Well, that's it for me." He swept his arms open over the baize, back and forth, like he was showing everyone his hands were empty. Mike, Jonas, Arlene, and I each tossed him a chip. Viet Nam looked around like we were all crazy. "Thank you all," Jimmy said, and then he was replaced by a woman who looked like she was some country singer's mom.

"Bets back," she said, and started shuffling.

"How you doing?" Arlene asked me.

"I'm keeping up. You?"

"Almost done."

"Almost done?"

"Yeah." She took a long draw on her cigarette and then, squinting through the smoke, gestured with it at Jonas. "You see that man over there? See that scar on his neck? I paid someone to do that."

I tried to sneak a look at Jonas's neck again. He was staring, bored, at Arlene, shaking his head ever so slightly.

"Me and J used to be married. But then one day I

thought, I've had enough of that sonbitch."

Neither Mike nor Jonas seemed to be paying much attention to what Arlene was saying, but I looked to them for a signal on how I was supposed to take it. Jonas flicked his eyes over at me, his expression utterly flat, then slid them back over to Arlene.

"What're you looking at him for?" said Arlene.

"I'm not," I said.

"You turned your pretty head and pointed it right at him. Were your eyes closed?"

"You're right. I'm sorry. So you had someone kill him."

"That's right. We were living in New Mexico at the time, and this guy cut J ear to ear and threw him in a tailings pit out by one of the copper mines and there he lay, dead as a dormouse. Except then he woke up and caught a ride to Varadero and they sewed him up. He couldn't remember his name or anything." She took another heavy drag on her cigarette. "I collected the insurance. He may have been worthless in life, but whooooo, J was worth something dead. One million. Beautiful."

"Doornail," said Jonas, bored.

Arlene sneered at him. "Shut up, *honey.*"

"Bets up, please," said the dealer. She was a lot less friendly than Jimmy had been. She dealt Arlene and Viet Nam aces off the top of the shoe, but she didn't say anything, didn't wish them luck. Gave herself a ten.

"So, what happened," I said.

"Play," said Arlene. The dealer laid both Arlene and Viet Nam blackjacks, but her down card was an ace and she took everyone's money. "When's Jimmy coming back?" Arlene asked her.

"Who?"

"The fat guy who knew how to deal."

"What're you complaining for?" said Jonas. "You lost."

"But on a blackjack? That's the wrath of God, J. I don't need that."

Viet Nam was arguing with the dealer. "Blackjack!" he was saying.

"Not if the dealer has blackjack too, sir. You don't knock on blackjack, house wins."

"No," said the old man. "Blackjack. Twenty-one."

The dealer tightened her yellow hair on the back of her head and started dealing another hand, but Viet Nam spread his arms over the table and wouldn't let her. This is one of those things you don't do at a blackjack table, and there were three guys on him instantly.

"Hey! Don't fucking touch him," Jonas said, trying to pull the security guards off the old man. "He doesn't understand."

"Well then, he shouldn't be playing."

I stood up and acted rational. "Is there someone here who can maybe explain to him in his own language? Do you maybe have someone here who can talk to him?"

Viet Nam was very upset. The security had him so his arms were pinned to the sides of his head, and his long pink arms stuck out of the sleeves of his jacket a couple feet above his hair. Anyone looking our way (and there were plenty of people looking) would have understood right away that the old man had been nabbed for cheating.

"I win!" he said to a pit boss when one appeared.

"I know," said the boss. "Hold on." A young man came and started talking Vietnamese. The security guys backed away. Viet Nam argued with him, but the young man went over the finer points of house rules with him and then must have asked him if he was ready to keep playing, because the old man sat down again.

"His name is Hao," said the young guy. "He understands now and he says he is sorry, he would like to continue playing."

"Can you tell him he doesn't have to hit to seventeen every hand?" asked Jonas. "He's queering the deal."

The young man talked some more to Hao. Then he turned to Jonas. "A man does not stand on twelve. A man plays to seventeen."

"What the fuck," said Mike. "He's losing more than he has to and he's making it hard for the rest of us. Just tell him: if I do this—" and here Mike chopped the air with his hand "—it means don't take any more cards."

The young man passed this on, and Hao chopped the air back at Mike and smiled.

"Good," said Mike.

The lady dealer had been taken off the table because of the ruckus. I imagine if something goes wrong at your table they take you into a back room and ask you to watch the videotapes with them. They can tell if you're in on something based on what you say about the tape, I guess. Some guy named Earl was supposed to deal now.

"Hey, Jim," I said.

Earl looked up sharply at me. "What?"

"Never mind," I said, and Arlene laughed. Earl started shuffling.

"That was super sweet of you, mister," she said. "Stepping in and solving the situation. Can I give you a kiss?"

"I'm married," I said.

"I don't want to blow you. I just want to give you a prize for using your brains."

"I want to hear the rest of this story. About you and Jonas."

She leaned across the two empty seats and kissed me lightly on the lips. "Jonas? Who's that?" Jonas smiled sarcastically at her. "Oh, him. My dead husband. Well, this is what happened. I figured he was gone for good and I got the money and I started living the high life. I bought the best beers, I got a satellite dish—the only one in the park, I'll let you know. I bought myself a hundred pairs of shoes, just about. But fuck I was lonely. And to be honest with you, I felt like I was no better than a murderer."

"That sure is interesting," I said.

"Bets up," said Earl, and he started dealing. Two businessmen came and sat in the empty seats between me and Arlene. The first couple hands went well for everyone. Earl bust off a sixteen, then stood on an eighteen, but he was facing nineteens and twenties across the board, including Arlene, who tossed him a five chip on the second hand.

"You're winning now and you're throwing tips?" I asked her.

"Just shut up."

The shoe was hot for most of us. I started doubling my bets and then cashed in some of my tens. "Colour coming in," Earl said, and he counted out my chips in sharp, swift hand movements. I'd always liked the ritual of chip-counting. Most dealers know the distance from their fingertips on the table to the arched underside of their palm in chip-widths and they can grab a pile of chips, chunk them on the table, and know exactly how many are there. These guys never make a mistake. Earl tossed me two blacks. Then he dealt another round. This time, Hao came up with nine against Earl's three. Arlene stood on her twelve, and Hao hit to fifteen. Mike chopped the air with his hand. Hao chopped back and busted his fifteen with an eight.

"Jesus! What is wrong with you?"

"He doesn't understand what you're doing," I said.

"The hell he doesn't. The little guy explained everything to him. Hey, Hao? We won't think any less of you if you don't play like a man. Jesus."

Mike busted after that and so did Jonas.

"Let's get something to eat," said Jonas. "Hold our spots?"

Earl tossed down two blanks and kept dealing.

The businessmen were doing fine, but they didn't seem

to realize they were in a public place with mixed company. They were talking about some strippers they'd seen that afternoon. It was bothering me on Arlene's behalf, but she wasn't noticing. A little time passed and everyone played silently. With the chemistry of the table different, no one but the businessmen felt like talking.

One of them said, "You ever had a shit that hurt?"

"Oh fuck yeah," said the other.

"I had one yesterday, thought I was going to split in two."

"You get more than a couple of those and I want you to go see a doctor. That could be bad news."

"Do you guys mind?" I said.

The one beside me turned. "Mind what?"

"We're not all that interested in your friend's anus."

Arlene laughed and doubled her bet.

Later in the evening it seemed to me that Arlene had lost pretty much everything, but then she pulled out a thousand more dollars and started playing with that. Jonas was shaking his head.

"There *is* charity, you know."

"What would you know about charity, asshole? Anyway," she said, turning to me, "it took J about two years to get his memory back, but when he did, he turned me in as fast as you can say jack shit. But they never could prove anything and I didn't do any time. So he was back in the park, and to be honest with you, I'd had a long time to think about what I'd done, and I felt awful. I also realized I loved the son of a bitch and I'd do anything to get him back."

"Well, it was good luck then that the murder didn't take."

"I suppose. I started sending him cards and flowers. Men like flowers, you know."

"I know."

"And I started cooking him dinners and taking them over and leaving them on his steps. And finally he let me in, and we started talking and I said to him, J, I still have four hundred thousand dollars. Let's you and me find some way to spend it together. But guess what? The idiot didn't want to spend his own fucking money. And he didn't want *me* to spend it, either."

"And he wants you to lose it all before he'll take you back."

"Bingo." She raised her eyes at Jonas. "I should've married a smart man."

She was betting a hundred a hand and losing it quickly. "I'm working to a plan," she said. "Our anniversary is in three months. I started four months ago. I lose about two and a half thousand a night, I worked it out. So, we get to spend this time together, you know, like dating, and at the end, I'll be plumb broke and we'll be together again." She smiled sweetly at Jonas.

"I just want you to know," he said to me, "that I don't know this woman at all, apart from here."

"You're such a prick," said Arlene. "I'll split that," she told Earl. She had a pair of fives.

"You know you never split fives, Arlene. You can double down, but I *do* have a ten," said Earl.

Arlene showed him her teeth. "Did you hear a word I was saying?"

"Yeah, but I have to help players through the tough hands if it looks like they don't know what they're doing."

"I *know* what I'm doing. I'm splitting." He hit her to seventeen on the first five, and she took a ten and a king on the second. He had twenty.

"I'm getting tired," Arlene said to me. "I don't usually split. It goes too fast."

"If you don't know her," I said to Jonas, "then what's that scar on your neck?"

"Trust me," said Jonas, "if I had a patch over my eye, she would have told you she'd paid someone to shoot me in the head. Honestly. I come here a lot, and she always ends up at my table and eventually she tells someone this fucking story. It's word-for-word most nights. I don't even listen anymore."

"See how heartless he is?" said Arlene. Earl dealt her a blackjack and gave her quite a bit of money. "This is ridiculous," she said. "I'm all in."

"Table limit's three hundred."

"Clear it, then."

Earl spoke to one of the pit bosses and then came back and told her she could bet her stake if she wanted to. Arlene pushed it all out in front of her. Earl dealt her twelve against his seven. I had a hard nineteen, Hao fourteen, Mike and Jonas both hard twenties.

"Odds are good for little ones," said Jonas to her. "Table's minus seven with all these tens. I'd bet on something small coming next."

"I have to hit anyway against a seven. Don't I, honey?"

"The hell with you," said Jonas. "You do what you want. Just when you've got that much money on the table, knowing the odds helps a little. That's all."

"Hit me," said Arlene, tapping the table. Earl dealt her a seven for nineteen. "Again," said Arlene.

"M'am, I really don't think you want another card."

"Hit me."

"M'am?"

"Are you deaf? Deal me another card."

"Look," said Earl. "I've probably got seventeen. If I was allowed to tell you what I had, I'd say, hey, I've *got* seventeen, I've got a ten and a seven, and I'm gonna have to stick with it. But I'm not allowed to tell you my hand, so all I can say is, I *probably* have seventeen. Nineteen would beat me in that case."

"You fucking dickhead. Hit me."

"There's no need—"

"HIT ME." Earl peeled an ace off the shoe. Jonas started laughing. "Hit me again," said Arlene. He busted her.

Mike and Jonas were bent over the table. Hao was pointing at his cards for a hit, but Earl was trying collect himself. He'd just seen Arlene lose fifteen hundred dollars. "Give Viet Nam a card," Mike said, wiping his eyes.

"What?" said Earl.

"Hao. He wants to hit to seventeen."

Earl dealt him a three.

"See?" said Mike. "That's the way you play like a man." He and Hao shook hands.

Arlene stood up. "I'm done," she said. "Are you coming with me?" She was looking at Jonas.

"She does this every night."

"Why don't you go with her?"

"Why don't *you*?"

"I'm married," I said.

"Well, so am I."

"Main difference between you two," said Arlene, "is that Jonas isn't off gambling behind his wife's back. Right, darlin'?" Jonas was shaking his head again. Arlene waited beside the table with her arm outstretched. "Are we going?"

"Every night I have to do this," said Jonas, and he took out his wallet.

"Bets up," said Earl.

"Do you have to be a prick?" said Jonas. "Just hold it for a second." Fear flashed in Earl's eyes as the pit boss glided past behind him. In a minute, it would be the video room for Earl. Jonas opened his wallet on the table and slipped out a thin sheaf of photos. They were department store studio shots. Twelve ninety-nine for the biggest package, but a rip-off because the colours always fade. A woman and two kids. "My wife," said Jonas. "Betty. My little boy, James. My older boy, David."

"You know," I said, "I'm a photographer. I can do this kind of thing for you, but much better quality. Just as cheap."

"Did you hear a word I just said?"

"I did."

"Say their names."

"Uh . . . Betty," I said.

"To *her*."

I turned to Arlene. "Betty and James and, uh, David."

"Did you hear that, Arlene? Did you hear those names?"

Arlene's facial expression hadn't changed. She came over and kissed Jonas on the cheek. I guessed from previous evenings he knew not to struggle. "I'll see you tomorrow, then. A hundred and fifty thousand to go, baby." Then she walked out.

Hao had brought his own wallet out, and he was spreading snapshots on the table. There were about fifteen pictures, all black and white, of old people and babies. Creased from being hidden in a shoe, or tucked into a hat. We all stood around looking at them.

I wanted to tell Jonas that I believed his wife. I believed Arlene. No one who acts that crazy can be anything but a victim of love. I collected my chips and cashed them in. I'd done quite well. As I was leaving, I called Linda on one of the pay phones.

"God, where are you?" she said. I pictured her sitting up in bed, terrified and alone in the dark. I saw her cross-legged, cradling her belly in her forearm.

"I needed to stop for a while," I said.

"I thought you were going to be home hours ago, Tom. I was worried sick."

"I'm two hours away. I'm getting back in the car." I heard her lie back down. "I'll be home soon."

"You can't do this. I have to depend on you."

"I know," I said. Hao went by in the background and waved a sheaf of bills in the air. What a real man does. "I'm sorry," I said. "Go back to sleep."

She breathed out, resigned, relieved. "Love you," she said, and hung up.

I had intended to tell her about all the money, but I thought it could wait. I got back on the road and started driving. The weather hadn't changed much, and the headlights of oncoming traffic grew into bright, wet starbursts in my windshield. I got off the main road and took a quieter, secondary highway. It was dark, except for the rain flicking into the brightness of my headlights. At one point, I was driving through the town I grew up in, where my father had once owned a hardware store. I went through the blinking stoplights, and passed the store, and my dead father was there unpacking bags of birdfeed from a cardboard box. Then I had to heave the car back toward the centre of the road and I drove the rest of the way home with all the windows down, the cold rain blowing through. The money was the only thing still dry when I got there.

COLD

I was going to Europe to meet up with an old friend whose life was falling apart, and my wife was unhappy about it. "Louis?" she'd said. "And who is this Louis?" It was hard to explain how a man I'd never mentioned before was now so important to me that I had to fly to Europe to be a friend to him. This unsuccessful conversation unfolded in many rooms, with me usually entering them second, in mid-sentence.

"—will still go one day. We will."

"But you're going now. To help an *old friend*."

"Why does that seem so heartless to you?"

"Fine," she said in a flat voice. She tilted her head at me and opened her eyes wider. "Is there anything else?"

"I don't think so, Carol."

"Then have a lovely time." I listened to her bare feet pad across the wooden floor in the foyer. She was the kind of person who could infuse her footfalls with reproach. I stood there, alone, breathing heavily.

"You'd understand if you weren't so bent on taking it personally," I said.

I decided to go simply because Louis was the kind of person who would never have asked for help. I was never called upon anymore for help or advice. I had no children, and at work—I owned a small business that custom-made insoles—the kind of aid I offered was rote and impersonal. When someone reaches out to you because they think you're their last chance, you really do have to go. And in any case, I hadn't been out of Toronto in three years.

Louis was flying in from Indianapolis, so we co-ordinated at Heathrow, where we were going to wait for a connecting flight. Louis came off the plane and he put his arms around me slowly, as if I'd bailed him out of jail. "God, Paul," he said, "this is what it's all about."

I stepped back to get a better look at him. He was older, and pasty from his American eating habits. But his hair was still a short sandy brown and his face was the same round, tired baby's face I remembered from our college days. He was wearing an Oxford blue button-down, but the collar was frayed a little, as if it had rubbed against his neck one season too many.

"Look at you," I said.

"Look at *you*!" He reached over and squeezed my upper arm.

We stood for a moment shaking our heads at each other.

"Hey, listen," he said. "I had an idea. I'm going to buy you a watch."

I held up my wrist. "I *have* a watch, Lou. It's a good one."

"No, no. Something special for the trip—just for the two of us, so that in all the pictures, we'll both be wearing our new fucking watches! You can throw yours out at the end of trip."

"You better save some of your money for alimony."

"I just want it to be *special*." He pretended to sulk. "C'mon. I'm buying you a watch."

He bought us identical black Swatches in the airport store. A single blue-black gem marked twelve o'clock, and a disk mounted over the top of the face showed the time by means of another gem. So it looked like two distant stars, one rotating at the edge of another.

We went to the British Airways lounge and waited for our flight.

"Let's synchronize," said Louis. "It's 4 A.M. local time . . . mark." He snapped the stem of his watch into place.

I did the same. "Mark," I said. I jarred the minute disk when I pushed the stem back in and my watch said 4:02. I turned my wrist away. The lady at the desk took up the PA microphone and invited the elderly and infirm on board.

There wasn't a lot I remembered about Louis. Back in Indiana, we'd become roommates by force of lottery; I'd got there first and taken the bed by the window. When he showed up, he unpacked about twenty identical white button-downs with breast pockets, so I had him figured for engineering before he even told me. He had two belts, one brown, one black, and he kept a comb on his shelf, nested in a hairbrush, just like my grandmother used to. There was a picture of his mother and one of his brother tucked into the upper corners of his mirror.

We didn't become fast friends, but we were each exotic

to the other, so a kind of common fascination took hold. He'd already decided he was going to marry his high-school girlfriend, Lorena, but I was having trouble getting past my third dates. (A goatee and an inclination to nervous laughter had something to do with it.) His steadfastness intrigued me. Lorena visited once a month, but he'd never get excited; it was as if they were already married. She'd come to the campus, hair all crimped, with a package of peanut butter cookies or else some sandwiches wrapped in waxed paper, things she'd made in her mother's kitchen in Elkhart, a four-hour bus ride away. She was horribly shy: if standing, she'd clasp her hands tightly in front of herself, as if she were naked. The three of us would make a few Carl Buddig corned beef sandwiches and talk about Elkhart before maybe watching a late movie, and then they'd sleep together in the other single bed, chaste as nuns. In the morning, he'd dry himself second on the only towel he owned. I could probably remember a few other things but there's not a lot that hasn't burned away. I don't even remember much of myself, or what I thought of my life then.

On the plane, I watched the sun rise and angle into Louis's face. He shuddered at it and turned his head down toward his feet. I figured out that he'd been married for almost ten years to Lorena, and I felt bad for him because it was over.

"So . . . you hanging in okay?" I asked him when he looked up.

"Oh, yeah." He smiled wanly and arched his eyebrows

out the window. "Looking forward to some brews and a bit of sightseeing."

"And you're feeling all right?"

He turned to me. I could feel the plane point down. "I just said I was."

In Geneva, it felt like you could walk through the door of any one of the bright shining buildings there and order just about any crime you felt like committing. Only the sight of blood gurgling up through the polished sewer gratings could have convinced me I was seeing the city's true face. The traffic police stood in little red-and-white-striped huts wearing cotton gloves. We saw one singing. It was sinister.

We got on a train and went to Basel, where I had some relations I'd stupidly contacted. The relations didn't speak English, and they gave us *spaetzle* with gravy on it. One night, an uncle (I think he was an uncle) told us his whole life story in German. Louis kept nodding politely and saying "Da . . . da . . ."—which was Russian, but it was enough to encourage the uncle forward.

On one afternoon, we went to a big museum and walked through it, our coats draped over our arms. Impressionists, all dappled light and big frocks. The women in the paintings looked well fed, like farm animals, and the gallery was packed with people speaking German and French. When we left, Louis said, "It was what I expected." He said that a few times in the first few days. Kind of let down, but big about it.

After the second day I stopped trying to draw him into conversation, and that bear-hug grandiosity he'd shown at Heathrow was gone now, too. He walked along with his hands shoved into his pockets, seemingly lost in thought. I wanted to ask him what he was thinking, but there was an air to him at times like this that I thought wouldn't have brooked interruption. Everyone has this side to themselves, some part they don't want you prying into. I have it, although obviously I was not the person, at this time, who needed prying into. I felt a little . . . *underused* might be the word, but I reminded myself that talking about your feelings doesn't come easily, even to some women, and Louis was getting to know me again. We did have a few laughs. He did his impression of a Swede trying to swear in English. "Eat my fuck!" he said, and we fell down.

We crossed into France and went to Avignon, where a big theatre festival had just ended. Playbills were blowing across the town square. I called Carol.

"You having a good time?" she said.

"It isn't about having a good time, sweetie. He needed me to do this for him."

"You're a big-hearted kind of guy."

"I'm looking at him right now," I said. "You should see him. He's hunched over a little cup of coffee about fifty feet from here. He looks sad."

"Well then, why don't you go back and cheer him up?" She put the phone down.

At the table, Louis looked up morosely from his coffee. "I never met your wife."

"Oh, Carol. She's a big-hearted kind of girl." Louis was sitting in his chair as if he'd plunged into it from a rooftop. "You know, I don't think I ever saw Lorena again after '87. She was pretty, I remember. Thin."

"Not always." He emptied a packet of sugar into his cup. There wasn't any coffee in it, though. "She went up and down, like a blowfish."

"Was her weight an issue between you two?"

He looked at me, his mouth screwed down at one side. "I don't remember. We can't stay here—" he raised his index finger to signal the waitress— "it's a fucking ghost town, and frog sounds like a head cold to me. I'll get this."

He wanted to go somewhere new, but I wasn't interested in Germany (I'd had enough of it in Switzerland), and he thought Italy was going to be mainly farms. We compromised and settled on Strasbourg, a mid-sized town on the border between France and Germany. Louis's guidebook described it as "a relatively sedate town with some lovely gardens." Avignon it had called "a town of famous bridges, from the songs of your childhood."

In the Avignon station, I bought a blank notebook, thinking I'd keep a diary. I hadn't written in a diary since I was a teenager (my last entry, from 1977, if I remember correctly, was *WHAT THE HELL IS HAPPENING TO ME?*) Already I'd seen some things and had some thoughts I wanted to remember, and I believed that if Louis saw me being contemplative he might start to feel like talking. I limbered up with a postcard on the train as Louis was getting us two Kronenbergs.

> *Honey—you'll probably get this after I get back, but I want you to know I'm taking notes for our trip. You'll love the south of France—it looks just the same as the paintings you like. We're on our way to Strasbourg now, which is supposed to have some nice gardens! Love you, Paul.*

The front of the postcard was that famous picture of two Parisians kissing. Funny how uncomfortable her hand looks, I thought.

Louis came back with the beers.

"You looking forward to Strasbourg?" I asked him.

"It's still frog, but I guess it'll do."

"They speak German there."

"Mm," he said. He flicked open his newspaper and folded it back. It was *USA Today*, and the front page featured a picture of an American bishop kicking a soccer ball. "You having a good time over there?" he said from behind the newspaper.

"Great," I said. "You?"

"Just like I thought."

I leaned across and pulled the paper down. "You keep saying stuff like that. Are you not enjoying this? We can do something else if you want."

"Naw, it's great, honest it is. You're going to love Strasbourg."

"How do you know?"

"It just sounded like you really wanted to see it."

I let the paper go and he raised it over his face again. *Louis seems different,* I wrote in the notebook. I looked up from time to time to see the fields and bridges and piles of wood speeding by. A couple of children waved at the train from a street in a small village. European children always seemed kind of grown-up to me. I wrote, *Louis has been acting like some other part of him is arriving in the next few days. He's a little boring, like he was when we were roommates.*

"What are you writing?" Louis asked.

"Just some stuff about travelling."

"Don't write shit about me in there."

I flicked the back of his paper. "I'm taking notes on your *condition*." He snorted.

In Colmar, a woman got on the train and sat down beside Louis, who was sleeping now, the newspaper crushed against his chest, his mouth open. The woman was wearing a yellow rain slicker, like the ones kids wear when you see them running for school buses. I guessed she was around thirty. She had a perm and wet brown eyes, and if you'd run into her on a train in Toronto, you'd figure she came down from Sudbury. But she was French, and the styleless perm looked fashionable on her. She wore a cornflower-blue cashmere pullover under the raincoat, and the two garments against each other seemed casually erotic, as though she'd stood in her closet that morning in her black underwear and thought about what might make her feel good.

It was nearing dusk, and we were getting closer to Strasbourg. Outside the train, the language of billboards was shifting back and forth. One showed the new Lexus and a woman in a bikini standing in front of it with her arms crossed. The caption said *Ne touchez pas. Sauf si vous savez ce qu'elle a besoin.* The next one showed Tony the Tiger. *Sie sind Schmackhaft!* he said.

The woman leaned across Louis and drew down the canvas blind to block the hard orange sunset. She looked across at me. *"Ça suffit?"*

"Uh, *oui* . . ."

"Pour écrire." I smiled dumbly, like a tourist, and she tried, *"Sie sind ein Schreiber?"*

"Angleterre," I said, accidentally.

"Oh!" she said. "You are from England."

"No, Canada. Do you speak English?"

"Oh yes, I do. Canada. There, the French people want to run away."

"Well, they need the money, so they're staying for now."

She nodded at that. It was nice to have said something really offensive without anyone shouting about it. Of course, I didn't really have any idea how I felt. The woman smoothed her raincoat down along her legs and smiled. I waved my pen, as if to say, *Well, back to work on my political writing!* since I couldn't think of anything to talk about, even though I wanted to. For some reason, in the four days we'd been in Europe, we hadn't had any interesting encounters—perhaps, I thought, because Louis looked so dark and unapproachable. The woman took out a paperback novel and opened it to some part near the end, and read, biting her bottom lip. I imagined that maybe she and I were married and heading back to our place in Strasbourg, and later she would tell me about her book, how the heroine escapes her beginnings, or some such thing. And that later, we'd be in the bath or looking over travel brochures, choosing between Ventemiglia or the Côte D'Azur for our holidays, and she'd say, *Do you want to wash my hair?* Although I also imagined her saying, *Did you clean the barbecue like I asked you to?*

Louis shifted in his sleep and the paper slipped out of his arms and onto her lap. She collected it awkwardly and folded it and put it back on the table between us.

"The news has putted him to sleep," she said.

"Mm. *Put* him to sleep. He's my friend, actually. Louis."

She held her hand out. "Janine."

"I'm Paul."

"And so, you are going to Berlin or Amsterdam, I guess."

"No—we were going to go to Germany or Italy, but we couldn't decide, so we're going to Strasbourg."

"Strasbourg!" She was delighted. "I *live* in Strasbourg! But why are you coming there? You have friends?"

"No, we just thought we should see it. Is that a bad idea?"

"No, no—only every year many people don't come to Strasbourg. I was surprised!"

The perm did look good, in some inscrutable French

way. I was thinking this as we kept talking. She told me about her work and where she was born, and some bike tours Louis and I could take from Strasbourg, and of course the big church, the Munster, which was the main reason to come to Strasbourg, unless you were going to school. When the train came into the station, she leaned over and woke Louis up by stroking his arm. He looked at her, displaced, then at me.

"Who the——?" he said.

"This is Janine," I smiled hard at him. "She's invited us to dinner."

When I first met Carol, I was at a St. John's Ambulance course at Our Lady of Grace, just down the street from where I lived. It was 1991 and I'd been single for so long I thought my face had started to scare women. In desperation, I started taking First Aid courses—a friend had met a girl that way. I figured that knowing how to save lives would be a quality really sensitive women would be able to pick up on.

When I arrived at the church, I saw Carol instantly. She was tall for a woman, and had hair on her arms, something I liked for reasons I still don't understand. At first we paired off into uncomfortable same-sex duos and did a certain amount of bandage-applying and pulse-taking. Above us, the Virgin Mary held her son and stared off into space. There really were a lot of things wrong with that picture, I thought, starting with the fact that it didn't even occur to her to keep him warm, or to put some pressure on those cuts.

I bided my time through the Heimlich Manoeuvre and self-applied choking remedies. (The apogee of single-hood: you're alone in your apartment and a piece of Salisbury steak goes down the wrong way, you find a chair and hurl yourself bodily against the back of it.) When it came around to drowning and shocking, I made my way over to Carol. I introduced myself and warned her I was both a bad swimmer and not that handy with small appliances, and she laughed. I could tell she thought I was harmless, and my heart jumped.

The instructor laid out her dummy and showed us where to place our hands on our partner's chest. Carol lay on the blue mat, with her hands by her sides, and I put my palm down below her clavicle and covered it with my other hand. I hadn't touched a woman since 1989. Carol took my hand and moved it up. "Don't break anything."

I pressed down, simulating heart massage.

"It's unlikely you'll ever have to do this," the instructor was saying, "since if you're alone with someone and you're doing CPR, it's probably all over but the crying. More likely, it's artificial respiration you're gonna need, and that's a skill you better get down."

I lay on my back and Carol put her hand under my neck, tilting my head back. "I hope you brushed your teeth," she said.

"I haven't eaten in a week, knowing this was next."

She put her mouth to mine and blew out a lungful of warm air. Her breath came streaming out of my nose, ten degrees hotter. I came up coughing and laughing. There were a lot of people laughing.

"Remember to pinch the nostrils," the instructor said, "and don't breathe for real—it's nasty."

"*Now* she tells us," I said. But Carol was just sitting back on her thighs with her hand over her mouth, laughing.

Strasbourg was lit up with flowers; more than I'd ever seen in my life in one place, although I'd never been to Holland and from the pictures I'd seen, Holland was worse. Louis put on his sunglasses and walked behind. Janine was singing. The whole place smelled like a potpourri.

"God, it's cheery here," said Louis.

"You have to let go all your bad energy," said Janine, walking backwards. "When it comes spring in Strasbourg, the students arrive for summer studies, and everything changes."

"I bet the average age goes down by five years," I said. "Ten."

"Tsh!" said Janine, and she linked her arms in ours. "You put your bags in my house and we will open a wine and make toast to the summer."

Janine lived above a store near the Munster. We walked up three flights of stairs and opened a door on a small, airy apartment. All the plants were alive. Louis walked slowly around and looked at things, flashing black in front of the windows, one of which was filled with the church in the square behind.

"You like Elmore Leonard?" he asked her, pulling a copy of *Swag* off her bookshelf.

"He is so sensitive," said Janine. "I think he is the best at the way people speak."

"I've never read him," said Louis. He laid the book down on a side table, like he was planning on borrowing it. Janine watched him and glanced over at me. I was sitting still, which seemed the polite thing to do, and finally Louis sat down as well, in one of her Ikea-style dining-room chairs. He leaned it back against a wall. "I've never had a home-cooked French meal before," he said, and Janine smiled and went into the kitchen and dumped frozen fish sticks and fries onto a cookie sheet. She put it in the oven and we waited, drinking wine. Janine smiled at us a lot.

"What is that song, 'Meilleur Ces Dotes'?" she asked. "There are some American students at the coffee shop who this morning were singing it, but I do not know it."

"What?" said Louis.

She sang a line.

"It's a song," I said. "Some nonsense song parents sing to their children."

"So it is for children?"

"Yeah. It's called 'Mairsy Dotes,' I don't know."

Louis leaned forward and the front legs of his chair came down. "It's 'mares eat oats and does eat oats and little lambs eat ivy,'" he said. "That's the song, it's not a nonsense song, only everyone calls it 'Mairsy Dotes' because it's cute."

"I had no idea," I said. "I always thought it was nonsense."

"Some people do."

Janine chiselled the dinner off the cookie sheet—it smelled fatty and rancid, but we ate it. She wanted to talk about American television. There were some people doing their doctorates on *Baywatch*, but we both said we never watched it. Louis stopped drinking wine and started drinking the beer he'd bought on the way. I gave him a sharp look when Janine was back in the kitchen, but he just shrugged. "I'm not a social-occasion person," he'd once said back at school. Whenever people got together in groups and started talking fast, he'd hang back. I'd forgotten he was like that. He also always accused me of being slick with women, which was utterly untrue, but I realized it was obvious that Janine liked me.

"Let's just go," I said quietly.

"We don't have to be rude."

"It's not rude. This isn't about making friends, you know—I thought we were here for you."

"Yeah, well . . . let's just set a while."

Janine came back in with a plate of digestive cookies. "You both have the same watch," she said.

"I bought them for us in the airport," said Louis.

"That is romantic."

She dropped two cookies on each of our plates. Her fingernails were painted a light silky blue I hadn't noticed before. We ate the dessert in silence. At eight o'clock, the church bells rang—eight heavy, deep gongs that made the windows rattle. "I live too close to the church," Janine said. "But it makes me feel safe."

Back at the hotel, we unpacked the clothes we wanted to air out for tomorrow. Louis stood in front of the hotel mirror, checking his face and squeezing blackheads, a disgusting habit he'd apparently never kicked. The sink was full of clothes. I lay on my back on the hard bed, the grease from Janine's dinner roiling in my gut. She'd kissed each of us on both cheeks at her door, sorry that we had to go and inviting us back to say goodbye before we left town. She kissed me on one cheek, and then the other, but the second kiss overlapped the corner of my mouth.

"*À la prochaine, écrivain,*" she said.

"What was that thing she told you?" Louis asked me in the cab.

"I don't know," I said. "I don't speak French."

At the mirror, his face angled up so he could see his chin close in the glass, Louis mumbled something about how the French and the Germans didn't make good bedfellows. He thought the architecture stank.

"Why are you so negative?" I said.

He grimaced in the mirror and wiped something off it. "I'm just saying."

"And you should stop that. You're lucky you don't have craters all over your face."

"From what?"

"Fucking . . . squeezing your face like that."

He ignored me and turned to look at the side of his

nose. We were up five floors, and there was a square of dusk in the window. In the building in front of the hotel, there were three big yellow steel cones attached to the building below the cornice. Transformers, maybe. They gave off an anxious hum.

"If you washed your face," I said, "your pores wouldn't fill up with garbage."

"Did you think, when we were in university, that people just pretended to like each other?"

"Why would they do that."

"You never know what people are going to turn into. You might need them one day."

"What does this have to do with hygiene?"

He angled himself away from the mirror a little and looked at me with a flat expression. "You don't think there's such a thing as social hygiene?"

"I'm losing you, Louis."

"I wonder if people thought you and I were just friends because we had to share a room. You think?"

He turned back to face the mirror, and I pushed myself along the bed so I could see his face again. His reflection was staring back. I was in an awkward physical position, half up on my elbows, but I held it because I had the odd sense that I had to remain still. Louis reached for a towel and now he was facing me. I sat up straighter.

"So, why did you come here with me, Paul?"

"Why? I came because you asked."

"You came to *help*." He dropped the towel in the sink. "I make you feel good about yourself, don't I?" His eyes were immobile. "I'm your country bumpkin."

"Look, Lou—I don't know where all this is coming from, but you've obviously been under—"

"Aw, forget it," he said, and he turned away and reached back into the sink where earlier he'd been washing a shirt with a wooden scrub-brush. "It's not worth it."

"That's not what—" I started, but I was cut off by the sight of his body spinning back toward me, his arm arcing around. I saw a thin stream of water trailing behind the scrub-brush before it cracked into my temple with the ringing sound of a golf ball being smashed off a tee. I flew back against the bed, my head assailed by a shrieking, car-alarm pain, and I lay there, panting, waiting for the rest of the assault, but nothing came. Maybe he'd slipped or had an attack of some sort? I looked over to him, lowering my arm slightly, and he was standing there frozen, looking at me with an expression that was somewhere between fear and rage. The side of my head was pounding.

"Lou?"

"What."

"Can you . . . go over into that corner, please?"

He looked to where I'd gestured and he walked over to it and stood there with his arms at his side.

I sat up and checked for blood. There was a hard lump with a dimple in it over my eyebrow. My hand was shaking. "Okay," I said. I kept an eye on him and stood up, moving for the door. I took my coat down from the hook.

"I'm taking the bed under the window," he said.

I nodded at him as I opened the door. "Okay, you go ahead then." I closed the door on his profile, his eyes still staring straight ahead.

"You cannot go back," Janine said. She'd put on a thin silk nightdress to come to the door and sat at the table beside me. She pressed a cold washcloth against my temple. "There is another room here."

"You're very sweet," I said, pulling my head away a little. Of course I wanted to stay. I wanted to forget about Louis. She'd made us tea and put a few more cookies on a plate, and I liked the idea of taking the teacup out of her hand and slipping her nightdress from her shoulders. I thought she'd probably let me, but it had been a long time since I'd taken any chances like that.

She lowered her arms to the table, and looked at the lights coming from the church. "It's vespers tonight. It makes the *quartier* smell like candles, and I think, when I am falling asleep, that it is someone's birthday!" She laid her head down on her arms and smiled sleepily. The dim light shadowed her sloping collarbone. "When I am a little girl, my mother made me a cake with coins in it of chocolate."

"That sounds nice," I said. "Once I had a pirate-ship cake."

She nodded. "Your friend is very sad."

"He might be crazy, too."

"Your poor head." There were tears in her eyes.

I got up to close a window because the tears made me feel odd, and I'd seen goosebumps on her chest. I couldn't remember the last instance in my life of that boyhood awe of thinking that a woman was actually naked under her clothes. It made me nostalgic for all that time when I still knew nothing. There were children in the street below, even though it was already dark. It seemed to me that they were safe, that their childhoods were going to be full of nothing but hot *pain chocolat* and fall vegetable soups and their fathers singing the classics at bedtime in cigaretty voices. I believed for a moment that when I turned around, I'd see what I was thinking of, Janine standing there with the lights from the church reflected in her eyes, her nightdress draped over the back of the chair. But instead she was collecting the plates from our tea, and she looked sad. I turned away from the look and saw the Elmore Leonard novel that Louis had taken out of her bookshelf, and I picked it up and slid it back into place.

"Will you go anywhere in the summer?" I asked.

"Where is there to go?" she said. "And with what person?"

"There's no one?"

She turned and vanished into the kitchen, hiding her face. "Oh, fuck," she said. She started running water. I stayed where I was; my hands were hot. I wondered where I'd spend the night, in what hotel, whether I'd call Carol or not. My ticket wasn't for another eight days, but even I knew it'd be wrong to keep travelling after all this.

"Are you okay?" I said.

She came out of the kitchen, her eyes brimming red. "I'm from Minneapolis," she said in a flat American voice. "I'm here on a French course. I'm lonely, what can I say?" She was standing there with her hands spread apart, suds dripping off them.

"You're from Minneapolis."

"I live in a two-and-a-half with my dog and my mother lives across the park with her lousy boyfriend and I got a BA from the U of M and my whole fucking life is in a three-mile radius," she said, hyperventilating. "So I came to France!"

She was wracked with sobs now, and suddenly it seemed to me that the perm really didn't suit her. I stood where I was and she slid down in the doorway. After a minute or two, she calmed down and brought her streaky red face out from behind her hands.

"Pretty exotic, huh? Meeting some French chick in Strasbourg."

"It's all right."

"You haven't had a very nice day, huh?"

"My day's been great," I said. I felt as thought someone had stuck a pin in my spine and left me unable to move. "Burnt fish sticks, physical assault, and a girl from Minneapolis."

She nodded, willing to accept my disdain. "I'm sorry." She pushed herself up and rubbed the corners of her eyes, took a deep breath. "Okay, so look," she said. "You liked me when I was French, and I'm the same person you were thinking of then, except for that one little thing. So, you know, stay, all right? We don't even have to talk."

My face was burning. "No thanks," I said, moving toward the door. *What Frenchwoman reads Elmore Leonard?* I thought. *How stupid am I?*

"Paul?" she said. "I really do like you. I wasn't faking that. Just stay a while, please."

"I can't," I said. "I have a headache."

At school, Louis had been a proponent of the world of concrete things. He thought every problem had an earthly solution. His hero was the guy who invented the intermittent windshield wiper. "Give me the coordinates and I can plot reality on a graph," was one of the things I remember him saying. I hated his certainty and I railed against it. We fought about physics—his god—because so much of it seemed boneheaded to me. Once we fought about heat and cold. "Heat is *not* the absence of cold," he said. He was sitting on his bed, collapsed there in the middle of dressing for a dinner thing, in a fit of exasperation. "*Cold* is the absence of *heat*. Heat is the result of a chemical or physical reaction. It adds something to the pre-existent condition. Which is cold."

"Is there cold when there's heat? No. So heat is the absence of cold."

"But when heat dissipates, Paul, you have cold. If cold dissipates, you only have more cold."

"Aha!" I said, "that means before it dissipated, there was *some* heat present. So the cold *is* absent."

He stared blankly at me, a dead-cow face. "You only

think you're making an argument. It sounds to you like you're saying something. But you're not." He looked at me in the way you'd look at someone it's hardly worth disillusioning. "You know?"

"Science thinks that because it invents the terms, it gets to define them into perpetuity."

"Are the terms we're referring to 'hot' and 'cold'? *Those* scientific terms?"

My jaw was tightening. Just a few moments earlier, it had felt like I knew what I was trying to say. "You know what this is like," I said. "It's like the way white Americans look at blacks. They see everything in context to themselves. It's pure solipsism."

"Can we just get back to heat and cold for a second? Let me put it this way." He got up slowly and reached for one of his all-white shirts. The resumption of dressing was a signal that the conversation was about to end. "When you leave a room—let's say it's a room with white *and* black folk in it—people say you're absent, although in your case they probably say 'Thank God!'"

"Ha ha."

"But when you come back in, they don't say your presence is the absence of your absence. Because that would be stupid. Either you're there or you're not. When you're there, you're heat. When you're not, it's cold."

The Munster was just around the corner from Janine's apartment, and people were streaming out of vespers, trailed by a mist of incense. The square was packed with students and supplicants. There were a few mimes, standing stalk-still under the klieglights, in suits and ties. I counted at least three of them, looking ridiculous and utterly alone, depending on the generosity of strangers to get them through.

I felt cold despite the mildness of the night and thought I'd better walk off my evening before going back to the hotel and calling the *gendarmes*, or whoever was going to get my suitcase for me.

I walked into the middle of the crowd leaving the church and fought the flow back to the doors. Inside, the stairwells were still open, and I slipped into one of them and climbed the long flights to the top, and stood at the stone wall there that lined the edge of the roof, under the carillons. It was about six o'clock at home; Carol was probably finishing her dinner—maybe one of her guilty-pleasure meals I won't eat, sardines on buttered toast, or boiled franks in macaroni—and getting ready to watch her programs.

Across the square on all sides, jumbles of terra-cotta roofs caught the moon at different angles and threw back a warm orange light. I had my hand on the wall, and on top of it and all across it, there were names scraped into the stone. Underneath my hand there was *Giuseppi, 1535*. All over, people had taken the time to leave signs of their pilgrimages—*Thomas Ames, Nov'r 1670*; *Maria, 1488*. I found a stone under one of the bells and scraped *Paul R, 1999*, but my name came out in a white powder. From the parapet, I could see small crowds surrounding the buskers, leaving them at the centres of little circles. A man's voice behind me said "*Nous sommes fermés,*" and I turned to look at him, but I didn't move. "*Monsieur,*" he said, coming toward me. I don't know why, but I backed away from him, and he stopped, and extended his hands cautiously. "*Monsieur? Écoute-moi, hein? Mon ami?* I talk to you!" I remained where I was, staring at the man who thought he was going to have to save my life. If I'd spoken his language, I might have been able to explain how I'd come to this moment in my life, but what people say about themselves is not nearly half of what you need to know about them. After another moment, I stepped back from the parapet and the man lowered his hands and smiled at me warmly. A misunderstanding is all it was.

THE VICTIM, WHO CANNOT BE NAMED

At first, on walking into his house, Peter Bowman thought his wife was laughing at a nature show. He saw the back of her head, and the screen in front of her flashed pink and black, and there were sounds of a pursuit. He came closer to where she was sitting, and heard that she was weeping.

"What are you doing?" he said.

"That's Vanessa," said Margot quietly. "It's Vanessa."

He saw that the image on the television was his daughter, a junior in high school. He grabbed the remote control and clicked the image away, and Margot collapsed into her lap. There was a bubble-wrap envelope beside her. It was addressed, in big Magic Marker letters, to Nessa Bowman. He picked it up; there was nothing in it.

He and Margot had been discussing Vanessa recently, an ongoing conversation about a child who was gradually becoming strange to them. There had been the changes in hair colour and the debatable fashions, but he and Margot were as enlightened about these things as they could be, and they didn't turn their concerns into *issues*. They placed their faith in providing a good house, with books and other wholesome diversions. There was nutritious food and opportunities for personal development—piano, swimming lessons. They knew rebellion would come, would rage through the house at some point, and they had faith that it would pass through without breaking anything that couldn't be fixed.

Peter had gone through an adolescent phase he remembered well, when he grew his hair long and made political pronouncements about things he didn't really understand. Feeling passionate about something seemed a defining rite. His parents hadn't taken it away from him, and he did not want to take it away from his own children. Whatever Vanessa was going through, he and Margot understood it was necessary, ordained by nature.

But *this*. Peter checked the envelope for a return address, knowing he'd find none, and then performed a moral calculation that would have resulted in Margot opening it. Opening the envelope was a transgression in itself, the sort of thing neither he nor his wife would normally do. He started with the name on the envelope, a version of "Vanessa" they knew no one to use for their daughter, then backtracked to the conversation the previous night about whether one of them should sit down with the girl and make sure everything was all right in her world.

He remained behind the couch. He knew he was supposed to sit on it with Margot and comfort her, or lead her out of the room and assert control in the way she might be expecting him to. But he did not do any of this. Rather, as if powerless, he tilted up the remote control feebly and clicked the TV back on. A ball of white light expanded and became Vanessa. There were two boys in the video with her. Peter and Margot watched silently, Margot with her hand over her mouth. The video showed their daughter involved in a variety of sexual acts, some of which Peter and Margot had both, at one time or another, enjoyed with each other. It was a display of knowledge as well as of sexuality, and it was hard for them to know what they were reacting to. Often, both of the boys were inside their daughter at the same time. When the tape ended, they both watched the white fuzz on the screen in silence.

"We have to show this to the police," Peter said, finally.

Margot shook her head.

"It's evidence," he said.

Margot took the remote from her husband's hand and silenced the hiss. "Rape victims don't smile, Peter."

Vanessa returned from her ballet class at six thirty. Her younger brother, Eric, had been home since five, and had walked around the house in complete silence, being aware (as children are) that asking his parents why they seemed so upset was only likely to result in a reaction, rather than any information. There was no dinner cooking. He eventually grabbed a bag of chips and went downstairs to play a video game that involved a dexterous fox retrieving a nuclear warhead. When Vanessa came through the door, she had time enough to offer only a sing-songy hello before Eric heard, in quick succession, the sound of someone slapping Vanessa, Vanessa crying out in shock, and his mother calling his father's name. He could then hear the three of them going up the stairs.

He returned to his game, not paying much attention to what was happening on the glowing screen in front of him, trying to behave normally. His was a family of rare outbursts, and both his parents worked in quiet professions—his father was a radiologist, his mother a librarian at city hall. At one time or another they had both expressed their belief that raised voices and anger never accomplished anything. Listening, observing, and other forms of stealth were their touchstones. Eric had once stood in the protected booth where his father's technician took the X-ray pictures, and he'd looked at the images afterwards. Milky shadow and solid white got resolved into some benign thing or another; sometimes the pictures confirmed something bad. No matter what the outcome, his father would lightly touch the X-ray, naming the thing-made-visible, and write it down on a pad. On the few times Eric had visited, his father had found a couple of tumours and a number of broken bones. *Here* and *here*, his father had said, showing him where the breaks were, his fingertip slowly tracing a bone.

That his sister had been hit by one of his parents was unimaginable to Eric. He cast his mind back over the things he'd done recently that he knew were wrong, but he couldn't come up with anything worse than smoking a couple of cigarettes. It was the kind of thing his mother wouldn't have approved of, but she would never have hit him for it. His father might even have given him one of those looks that said he was surprised to discover his twelve-year-old was smoking, but that it improved him somewhat by its daring. Although, of course, he could be *compelled* to stop, and he would stop.

The only thing he could be certain of was that whatever Vanessa had done, it was worse than smoking.

In her room, his sister sat alone on the bed, her hand pressed against the hot spot on her cheek. She pushed back to create more space between herself and her parents, who stood just barely inside the room.

"What's the matter with you?" Peter said. "Do you have any idea how dangerous this is?" He waited a moment, already exhausted from the effort of his anger. "Your mother and I are completely stunned. And disgusted. Who ever taught you to behave like this?"

Vanessa watched her mother, whose thoughts she believed she could read, but her mother lowered her head. "Tomorrow," said her father, "we're going to Dr. Davies and he is going to run every test known to man on you. But before that, you're going to give me the names of these animals and any other information you have about them."

Vanessa stared sullenly at her father.

"Do you have anything to add to this conversation?"

"I don't know their names."

"Should we play this tape for your friends? Maybe they know."

"Maybe they do."

This sass provoked Peter, and he lunged toward her, but Margot shouted his name and he stopped himself. "Get out of here now," she said.

"I want an answer!"

"What does it matter?"

"You can't bring the anonymous to justice." He turned to his daughter. "You try to remember the names of these boys who *raped* you."

When he left the room, Vanessa started to cry. Her mother did not come and sit beside her as Vanessa thought she would, but remained beside the door, watching her, waiting her out. After a few moments, seeing her tears were having no effect, Vanessa calmed down. "*Were* you raped?" said Margot.

"I don't know!"

"Whose camera was it? Who shot it?"

The girl drew the back of her hand over her mouth. The fear she'd been feeling from the first slap had grown into a general sense of danger. Her mother might even be more difficult than her father. "It was on automatic," she said.

"Whose camera?"

"I don't know."

(In the hallway, her father leaned against the wall opposite, his mind reeling with strange geometries, picturing the camera placement, the size and shape of the room, the various alignments needed to minimize shadows, then shook his head to loose the figures rampant in it.)

Margot went over to her daughter's television, now a sinister presence. They'd bought it for her as a gift for earning straight A's the previous fall. Margot held the tape up. "How could you let them do this to you? How could *you* have done this?"

"I don't know."

"That's the last time you're going to say that, Vanessa. You obviously knew very well what you were doing." She was not going to cry in front of the girl. "I feel I don't even know you. How could a child of mine—?"

"Mum—"

Margot turned sharply and kicked the television set off its stand. It struck the wall and then the floor, sending up a shower of blue sparks. Immediately, Peter opened the door and looked back and forth between the stand, and his daughter and wife. Margot was shaking her hands in front of her, as if trying to dislodge something from her fingertips. "They weren't even wearing condoms!" she said to her husband.

"Mum—"

She rounded on the girl, her eyes red and furious. "You could be pregnant, for Christ's sake!"

"They didn't come *in* me."

"My god—"

"You could have AIDS," said Peter. "Have you thought about that?"

"They aren't gay."

"I'm not even going to respond to that."

"So you *do* know them," said Margot.

"Does it look like we're strangers?"

Margot held her tongue and just stood there, trying to breathe. "Who's seen this tape?" she asked.

"We all have a copy."

"You think if you each have a copy that'll keep everyone honest?"

"I don't know," said Vanessa. "They both wanted one."

"Naturally."

When they were going out, as students at the University of Toronto, Peter and Margot had developed a ten-year plan. There was travelling to be done and degrees to be finished. They were both twenty-one, and Peter was going to specialize. Margot could wait until she was thirty to have kids—it was getting to be safer to have children later—and that way, they could enjoy what their own parents called their "youths," and do the things some friends of theirs regretted not having done before starting a family. They even wrote it all down, with dates along the top and rows playing down the side, with headings like *Destinations*, *To Buy* (a car in Year Two, a house in Year Five), and *Money Saved*. Then Margot got pregnant three years in. By that point, they'd bought a car and driven to Orlando in it. The rest of the plan went fallow. By the time Vanessa was born, what they'd thought they were going to do didn't seem to matter: reality had usurped fantasy. They adjusted to the possible, and they liked it. Year Eight would be Eric, this time planned.

Vanessa slept in their bed for the first year, a bump of warmth between them. To make love, one of them would change places with the baby, and sandwich her snugly between pillows. It was quiet lovemaking, sensible lovemaking. They got over feeling guilty. Margot found an article that said the smell of the pheromones and the rocking of the bed produced an especially sound sleep for a baby. Plus, she said, how could an infant resent the very thing that had brought it into the world?

When they tried to move Vanessa into her own bed, she resisted. For months, they struggled with her bitter night-cries, and if the two of them sat together watching television, Vanessa would not settle down until she was between them.

The solution in the end was a smaller crib, one that would allow the baby to feel enveloped. Many years later, Peter read about a woman who had developed a special machine that you lay down in, and it hugged you, and he thought about their solution to Vanessa's loneliness.

The night of the videotape, Margot and Peter lay together in the king-size bed, trying to follow the nightly ritual. Vanessa was in her room, forbidden to go anywhere but the toilet. They could hear her through the wall that separated her room from theirs. That such plans had been hatched only inches from their sleeping heads. How was it that she had not shot up in bed, as if from a dream, Margot thought, the moment her daughter had decided on this course?

The news played in front of them, the volume down to its lowest setting. It was Peter's habit to turn the news up if there was anything he thought he wanted to know about. The rest of the time he grazed business and news magazines and looked up only once in a while. He could sense a fire burning silently on the screen, or an update from a faraway war. Margot took her news with breakfast, and usually only from the newspaper, preferring not to be distressed by what was happening halfway across the world right before she went to sleep. She was a novel-reader, and each publishing season she bought the crop of new hardbacks, which she kept stacked on a low shelf beside the bed. She'd read half of something, then start something new, returning to the first book only when she was ready, when she had processed whatever it was that had made her stop reading it. As a librarian, she could have access to any book before the public, but she was a believer in paying for her pleasures, and they could afford it.

The night before, she'd been in the middle of three books. One was about some men on a misbegotten fishing trip, another was a family saga rooted in the New England of the pilgrims, and the last was an arty romance about a painter. A struggle anchored each one; like every good book she'd ever read, something dreadful was the occasion of every story, something to overcome. That was the nature of all books, although the stories of people's lives, as they were lived, weren't really like this. People tended to move forward motivated not, in the main, by crisis, but by ambition and hope and need. Most people she knew who suffered through terrible crises did not turn out to be more interesting, as they did in novels, but rather withdrew from those around them and only turned up again somewhere down the road, changed in a fugitive way that it was best not to talk about. Death was immune to this pattern, unless it was a shameful death, like a murder or a suicide, or someone who'd died from an avoidable health problem. Usually, death was made congenial by neighbours and friends. Later, grief could be difficult, but there was never any shame in it.

Margot made a pretense of reading the fishing novel. It took place in Spain. It really had more in common with the romance novel than anything, except that the part of the woman was played by the fish.

"What," said Peter.

She'd laughed bitterly to herself. But she shook her head. He turned the television off.

"I think we should keep her out of school for the time being," he said.

"I think so as well."

"You take her in to Richard tomorrow. I called him at home and asked him to run a pelvic series. He knows what to do."

She sat up. "Does he know why?"

"No. I just asked him to give her an appointment. He won't have any questions."

"How do you know?"

"It's the way I asked: He'll just do it and then you can bring her home."

He turned and switched off his lamp, muttering *Jesus Christ* under his breath. Her lamp threw a pool of light onto her hands and the sheets. She flashed on the image of a surgical procedure.

"Is that all?" she said.

"What else is there?"

"I don't think we should do anything that could take this out of our hands. I don't want you to talk to the police."

He said nothing, just dug himself deeper into the mattress. She put her hand on his shoulder and tried to pull him around to her so she could see his face. His stillness upset her. He'd always said he was good in emergencies, and it was true. He had a centred calm that was good for frightening moments. It was what made him a good doctor. But she didn't need that right now. She believed their daughter had made a mistake, but Margot wanted it to remain under their roof, where their own laws reigned. "You're going to make things more difficult, Peter. What are they going to tell you at this point anyway?"

"They're going to tell me what my rights are."

"*Your* rights?"

Now he turned around. His face was red, as if he'd been hanging upside down. "Get her to Richard Davies and then bring her home," he said.

Peter stayed in the bedroom the next morning until he heard Vanessa and Margot leave. Eric was downstairs, putting dishes away. Peter got dressed slowly; it felt as if he was being watched while he did it. His arms and legs didn't move the way he was used to, and he caught his breath once or twice. He went downstairs and said nothing to Eric while he folded a piece of white bread around a slice of cheese. Then the two of them silently gathered their things—he his briefcase, and Eric his books and baseball things—and got into the car.

Peter usually drove his son to school in the mornings, picking up another boy on the way, the other parent bringing Eric home. They drove over to the boy's house, and Eric stared into his baseball glove most of the way, looking up now and again to stare out the window with purpose, as if indicating there were things on his mind, too. Peter pulled into the boy's driveway and put the car in park.

"There's a problem in our house," Peter said.

"I know."

"It's a serious problem, but we're going to take care of it. You don't have to worry."

"I'm not worried," said Eric. Peter ran his hands down the side of the wheel, as if admiring it. "What's the problem?"

"I'm not going to talk about it. And if you hear anything at school, you're not going to respond. People are vicious. You stay out of it."

"Okay."

Peter looked at Eric steadily. It was not a look Eric had seen before. His father's face was still, but his eyes were as sharp as starlight. "This is *our* problem, do you understand? When families get into trouble, they have to work it out. It happens to everyone."

"I know," said Eric.

"You're a good boy, though. All right?"

Eric opened the door. "Does Vanessa have to leave school?"

"Go and get your friend," Peter said. "Everything is going to be fine." He watched his son go up the walk to the boy's house and trade a couple of words with the boy's mother, words he couldn't hear, that floated up into the air above them all and vanished. The friendly time of day, how distant that kind of thing seemed to him now. The boy emerged, another twelve-year-old, with a baseball bat that had a glove balanced on its tip. He watched the two of them come toward the car. He'd been a good father to this child, he thought, and images went through his mind of all the things he'd taught him. But they were the same things he'd tried to teach Vanessa. How to play fair. To have respect for the natural world. To develop a sense of wonder and joy (to use the terminology of the parenting books he and Margot had read). Maybe Vanessa had taken a different message from him? Did he somehow send her down a path different from the one he'd always thought she was on? He worked the seam of these thoughts for the fault, for whatever would show him where he'd even just slightly broken faith with the girl.

When he got to work that afternoon, X-rays from the morning's patients were waiting for him on his desk. He took the first group and slipped them into the wall viewer. A man's torso, the ribs arcing back into shadow, the organs behind dully arrayed. The body, reduced to the barest of structure, had no power to scandalize, he thought. You could show skeletons fucking, and it would never bother anyone. He leaned into the glowing pictures on his wall, his hand braced against the side of the light box, seeing the striations of cirrhoses on the man's liver. The story the body told. Anonymously, it was phenomenological, a statistic, a likelihood. With flesh on it, it was a man's death. In the rest of the envelopes on his desk, he would find a woman's death, a parent's relief, a child's ruination.

That morning he'd spent some time in the company of the police.

He'd gone to the station on Dundas and waited on a cold moulded-plastic chair in the waiting area. It was merely the strip of floor in front of the main desk, behind which men in uniform scuttered back and forth with papers in their hands. There were posters for missing children, some of them aged by computer. Another poster advised which types of freshwater fish you were allowed to catch in August, a month that was a whole season in the future.

His name was called and the little wooden gate held open for him and he was admitted to the back. He met Detective Stone, a large man in his fifties with grey stubble that curved down off his face and onto his plush neck. The detective ushered Peter into an interviewing room and slapped a fresh pad of legal paper onto the table between them. There was a wall-length window that looked out on the hallway, and officers walked past it, singly, or with someone who might have their hands behind their back, the officer leading them by the elbow. Peter sat cautiously, taking care not to let the videotape make a sound against the chair. He was carrying it in an inside coat pocket.

"Where's your daughter, Mr. Bowman," said the detective.

"She's at the doctor with my wife."

"Rape kit."

Peter nodded once.

"When can she come in, then."

"I'll find out."

Someone knocked at the door and stuck his head in. Stone looked up and nodded, then looked back at Peter. "Does she know her attackers?"

"They weren't really attackers," said Peter. "They're boys from her school." The detective wrote it all down. "They filmed it."

"The boys who attacked her."

"Yes."

"How do you know this?"

"I have the tape," Peter said, and instinctively he held it closer to his body. Detective Stone noticed this and tilted his head to one side, looking at Peter's coat. "I'm uncomfortable about this."

"Yes," said Stone. "We'll move to a better room."

He led Peter into the basement of the station. As soon as they'd come down the stairs and the sounds of the work day faded, it immediately seemed that this was a more serious business. For the first time, Peter became aware that there were fewer options for him now, fewer ways to think about all this. He was in a police station, therefore anything with the taint of crime on it would be brought forth as a crime.

The room in the basement was more remote, but there was a window in the wall. There were ten or so chairs in the room, and a television on top of a metal trolley. Peter sat in one of the chairs, but then stood again when the detective didn't take a seat himself. Stone put the tape in and pressed play. Peter turned toward the window. His hands started to ache, as if he were holding something very cold. He heard the sounds of the tape.

A couple of officers passed by the window and made eye contact with him and then quickly glanced at what was on the screen. How easy it was to put it all together. After a moment longer, Stone switched the machine off. Peter breathed in deeply.

"Your daughter's seventeen," the detective said.

"Yes."

"And who are these boys?"

"I don't know."

Peter stood uncomfortably, the window in his peripheral vision now filling more regularly with officers going past. It was change-of-shift, or lunchtime. Stone ejected the tape.

"I'm going to have a technician produce some photos from this. Just of faces. You can pick up the tape later this afternoon. Then we'll see." Peter watched the detective slide the tape into an interdepartmental envelope he picked up off a pile on a desk behind the television stand. The envelope was covered with signatures. You could see the tape through holes punched in the envelope. "Don't worry," said Stone. "Our guy has to look at this kind of thing all the time. He knows it's sensitive."

"Thank you," Peter said. He went out of the room and then up and out of the station. No one accompanied him.

As the afternoon passed, and the steady flow of patients came in and out of his office, Peter found his mind tuned in to what he imagined Detective Stone was discovering. Perhaps a computer program was comparing the images from the film with pictures taken by the Department of Motor Vehicles, or the Transit Commission, which had probably issued the boys' student cards. Maybe it was going to be that easy, just connecting the dots. He could be walking into Vanessa's school with Stone in a matter of hours, the detective already armed with names and the principal cooperating. They'd collect the criminals and bring them back down to the station and they'd be photographed and fingerprinted. It wouldn't take long before they realized what kind of long-term trouble they were actually in. And he, Peter, would watch it all in silence, his face a warning to the rapists that the longer their incarceration, the safer they'd be.

It took most of the afternoon, through a broken tibia, a fatty liver, a spot on a lung (a biopsy ordered), and a green-stick fracture for Peter to weave the entire story. After his last patient, he sat alone at his desk and savoured the possibility of punishment. The cars in the doctors' lot below had dwindled to fewer than ten. His nurse came in. "Do you need anything?" she asked.

"No," said Peter. "I'm just going to finish this." He put a hand down on his paperwork.

She stood in the doorway, looking at him. She was in her stockinged feet now. "You okay, Peter?"

"I'm great," he said, and he smiled at her brightly.

"I'll forward your calls to this line."

At Richard Davies's office, Margot had been asked to wait for Vanessa outside the examining room. The doctor took about half an hour with the girl and then sent her out smiling. Margot went into Davies's office and sat down in front of his desk as he washed his hands at his own sink. The washing of hands always struck Margot as a gesture of propriety. Her own father had washed his many times a day, before meals, after meals, when coming in from outside. It always seemed a quality of probity: a man who washed his hands could be trusted because he was thinking of other people when he did.

Richard Davies asked her about herself and Peter, and about the back extension on the house, which had been done some years ago, the last time he'd spoken to either of them. (Margot searched her memory for the difficulties—if any—they'd encountered on building the porch. All she could bring to mind were the picayune disagreements she'd had with her husband about paint colours and a sun-light; she hoped a time would come soon when such things would seem important again.) Davies opened Vanessa's file and looked down at it. Vanessa was a wonderful young girl, he said, but he thought she should be on the pill.

Margot nodded, feeling quite mute. She felt that, perhaps, he was letting them both off easy.

Davies led her out of his office with a comforting hand under her elbow, and kissed her on the cheek. He gave her a prescription.

"But what about the goddamned exam?" Peter asked when Margot told him all this.

"She's fine, he says."

"What does that mean?"

"He said physically she looked fine. There were no abrasions, no cuts. There was no evidence at all that anyone had forced her to do anything."

"So his answer is to put her on the fucking *pill*?"

"Peter."

"Did he suggest we advertise her services in the newspaper, too?"

There was silence on Margot's end. She was at a pay phone in the mall; she'd taken both kids out for dinner, to give a sense of carrying on—as much for her own benefit as for theirs. "We had a good day," she said quietly. "Vanessa and I."

"I'm glad."

"I'm not any happier about this than you are, Peter. But I've started to think—"

"What."

"We should be careful not to overreact."

"*Over*—. Where are you?"

"We're at the mall. We're having supper."

He had his thumb and forefinger on his brow and he massaged it hard. He stretched the skin so hard it felt as if it might split. "Well, why was your day so good, Margot?"

"We talked. I asked her if she was okay. Apart from this. I asked her, like we said we would."

"And."

"She didn't say a lot. But I had the impression that there's nothing really wrong. She's happy."

"She told you that."

"No. But she's not ashamed of herself. She's upset, I think, that we're upset. She told me she was glad we'd never been secretive about sex. That we'd always said it was healthy. Because she wasn't afraid."

He could hear her crying, almost silently, her breathing shallower now. "Well, I guess that makes us good parents," he said. "Doesn't it? She has such a healthy attitude."

Margot collected herself. "I have to go. When are you coming home?"

"I have more to do."

Behind her, in the mall, he could hear the spiralling

calliope of mall music, the threads of fine-clothing music, the ice-cream music. The voices of children and the sounds of coin-operated animals. He saw Margot standing in a hallway that led to lockers and a bathroom and his two children eating off of plastic trays. Were they in her sightlines? Could she see what they were doing, who they were talking to, who was, perhaps, looking at *them*? In his mind's eye, he went up over all their heads, into the barn-like girders that flew into the atrium above the food court, and he pictured all the people there, moving from their seats back to their cars, or entering the building, their shopping lists hidden in their pockets. And he saw the shape of their movements as solid lines showing where they'd been, and dotted lines showing where they were going, and the place was a hive of possibility. *Anything* was about to happen. There would have to be lines for eye contact too, and even thoughts. Everything was connected to his children, to his wife, to him.

"Did you go to the police?"

"I'm going to finish this up and come home," he said.

"Peter."

"We'll talk about it when I get home." He closed a file on his desk. He'd just signed a letter that ended with the words, *Thank you for referring this genuinely pleasant young man to me.*

"I want you to think more about this. About what Richard said. She's seventeen. Lots of kids her age are sexually active."

He slapped the desk with his palm. "That's not the

goddamned point, Margot! That's not the point!"

"Yes, it is!" she shouted back, and immediately lowered her voice. He imagined dotted lines converging on her in the hall where she was standing. "The point is that she's not a child anymore, Peter. The way we've learned that hurts us, but it doesn't change the fact of it."

"I have to go," he said, and he hung up.

It was fully dark when Peter arrived back at the police station—a spring darkness, shot through with fragrances. The light from within the station was welcoming, making it seem like a place of succour or refuge. Detective Stone was on the desk and asked for someone to cover him when he saw Peter. He opened the little gate and gestured to the first room they'd sat in, earlier that day.

"Can I get you a coffee?" he asked.

Peter shook his head no and the detective turned and looked at the man who was now the duty clerk and gave him a half-wave. He waited for Peter to go through the door before entering and sitting across from him sideways, his hip to the tabletop. A few police officers passed by the window, and some of them looked in. It seemed to Peter that they knew him. He was no longer a citizen come to the police to learn something, or to report something. He was a case. They knew him.

Detective Stone opened a new file folder between them, and there were three or four blown-up print-outs of the two boys in the film, their faces degraded by enlargement. Peter imagined for a moment that these were pictures taken after an interrogation, the faces swollen with what it had taken to get the truth out of them. Stone spun the file around to Peter and Peter carefully drew the pictures toward himself. He looked back and forth between them. He lay his finger lightly on the picture of the bigger boy.

"Who's this one?" Peter said.

"I can't tell you his name."

He looked up at the detective. "Why."

"He's a minor."

"What about this one?"

"That one as well."

Peter lowered his eyes back down to the report that he'd revealed by sliding the pictures out of the file. He saw his daughter's name and his address, and then, below it, the words *Juvenile A* and *Juvenile B*. He stared hard at those denominations, and the masks of the degraded faces on the pages in front of him. Detective Stone slid the file away from Peter and turned it around. "You can charge a minor, but their names are protected."

"She knows their names."

"*I* know their names. But this one," he pointed to the second boy, "he's fifteen. This one's sixteen. So I can't tell you anything about them."

"What if they're tried in adult court?"

"Their identities would still be protected. And in any case, before you try them, you have to charge them."

"I'm charging them."

The detective swivelled his big frame around in the

chair to face Peter. He closed the file and put one big hand over top of it. "Well, that's a problem. Since your daughter is of age, she becomes the complainant. You can't press charges on her behalf. She can, or we can, and—before you say anything—we have to feel a crime's actually been committed."

Peter stared at the closed file. He didn't want to annoy the detective. He thought if the detective said anything else that it could lead to a bad turning. So he stood up. "Well, I ought to talk to my wife and my daughter, then. I didn't know."

"Please sit down, Mr. Bowman. I don't think you understand everything yet."

"It's up to my daughter. I understand. My wife and I will sit down with her."

"Mr. Bowman, if your daughter presses charges, two things will happen. One is, these boys' parents will get lawyers, and the first thing the lawyers will do is lay countercharges. They'll say your daughter coerced *them*. But let's say, for whatever reason, they don't press their own charges. It'll go to court, and if the media covers it, and they will, the boys won't be named—but your daughter *will* be."

"Detective Stone—"

"I'm sorry, but that's the way it would work here."

"You can't tell me there's been no crime committed! You know boys, I'm sure you see kids like these . . ." he gestured hopelessly at the closed folder. "Look, Vanessa may be seventeen, but she's a child. And anyone who would let themselves be *used* like this would have to be—"

"Like I said, Mr. Bowman, the facts of the case—"

"There are two of them! They fuck her *up the ass*! You're telling me if they'd done this to her four months ago, when she was sixteen, that I could have laid charges?" The detective remained silent. Outside, in the hall, men swept silently past the window. No one had looked in when Peter raised his voice. He was alone with the facts of the case.

"There's only one thing that's actionable here," Stone said, "and unfortunately, it would be brought against your daughter. I'm not *going* to do that, but if someone walked in here and told me to make an example of someone, it'd have to be your daughter. And if either of these two boys' parents wished to, they could bring a charge of statutory rape against her." He waited a moment. Peter's mouth had closed to a thin white line. Finally, he sat down again. "Statutory rape is a charge that pertains to sex with any minor," the detective continued. "It's called statutory because it's deemed a minor cannot consent to sex, and therefore, the law calls it rape."

Peter's voice was thin. "I came in here to . . . how can you tell me there's nothing I can do? That it was *her* fault?"

"It's no one's fault, Mr. Bowman. That's what you have to understand. There was no crime committed."

Peter stood up and shoved the table back. Stone quickly flattened his hands against it to prevent it from striking him, but otherwise he remained still. Neither man spoke for a long moment. Then Peter said, "I'm her father."

"Yes," said Detective Stone with a single, emphatic nod.

"Do you have kids?"

"One of each."

"Me as well. I have a twelve-year-old son. What am I supposed to tell him?"

The detective stood up and swept the file to his side. "Don't tell him anything. It's none of his business." He waited a moment to see if Peter had anything else to say, and in his silence began to leave the room. "I'll tell you one more thing, in case it's something you're thinking of, Mr. Bowman. If you force your daughter to press charges, I won't be able to prevent anything that happens as a result. And there's a good chance that this will be the last time for a long time that anyone feels like talking to you." He went out the door. From the hallway, he said, "See the clerk. He'll have your tape."

When he finally came home, it was past midnight, and Peter went into the house silently and sat downstairs in the dark. He held the tape in his hands, this tape that now felt as if it could broadcast itself throughout the city.

Margot was in bed and so was Vanessa. Peter had gone downstairs, thinking he wanted to watch Eric sleeping. He went down into the basement, remembering the times when Vanessa was a baby and he'd get home after bedtime and go into her room to watch her sleep. The fragile lids under which her eyes would be flicking back and forth, the parted lips.

But what if once or twice he'd taken the precaution of stripping a bit of that simple safety away? By frightening her awake, or pinching her hard enough to bring her out of the warmth of sleep? Then maybe she would have had the sense not to film herself having sex with two boys. What on earth could help him trace the contents of that tape back to the quietly soughing child under her covers?

When he got to Eric's room, he heard the sound of the boy's television from behind the door. The telltale sounds of cartoon lasers, the muffled cries of imaginary victims. He turned away and went silently up the stairs again.

In the living room, he put the videotape into the machine and turned the television on. He quickly muted the sound and waited for the old VCR to thread the images on the tape through to the TV. It was now at a spot near the middle of the tape. Someone had watched it that far. In the scene now playing, his daughter was performing fellatio on the two boys, alternating between them. From this scene they would remove their T-shirts, and she her underwear. Then would come the myriad sex acts. In silence, it was a sinister dumbshow.

He brought himself to look at his daughter, really look at her. He looked at the body that he sometimes, and with some shame, imagined under her clothes. Did she look like her mother, he sometimes wondered, and here he saw that she did, a little. But who she really looked like was him. She had his long, greyhound torso, his gangly limbs.

The top of her pelvis poked out as his did, both of their flesh insufficient to contain their wild, oversized bones. In whatever way such an alchemy could be worked, it was his body on the television, except that it was his body as a young girl's. He felt the pained affection he'd felt for her when she was a child, aware of how delicate all of her was, and how tenderly he loved that frailty. What genius there was in nature, that it could tell him that even at this moment, when he was frightened and disgusted, this was still his child, the same one he had so instinctively wanted to protect. This was him, cut loose from the moorings of his being, and flung heedlessly into hers. But that did not make her separate from him.

He turned off the TV and went out to his car. In the station's interview room, he'd taken care to note the address of the boy called Juvenile B. The typed report had been exposed long enough for him to memorize it.

The fifteen-year-old's house was not far from Vanessa's school, although it was in the opposite direction from their house. It was now almost three in the morning, and when Peter got to the house it was dark. He parked the car across the street and killed the lights and engine. For five minutes he sat there in complete stillness, his hands palms-down over his knees. No cars went up or down the street, and nothing changed inside the houses that he could see. There was no one even watching television, no telltale dancing blue light. There was a jittery tension in his body; he gritted his teeth and could not relax his face.

The neighbourhood he'd come to was a mirror image

of his own: he felt the people who lived in these houses would have been people he'd be comfortable with, if he met them at a school function, a barbecue, or a school play. He knew what kinds of cars would be in those garages, which magazines came to the houses, which newspapers. The fifteen-year-old's garage door was not open. (You did not fear your neighbours in such quarters, only that, if you did something such as leave a garage door open, you would stand out. Not just to thieves, but to those around you. You did not want to advertise that you were blasé about your possessions, or careless. These solidarities were the shibboleths of such neighbourhoods.)

Peter tried the front door of the house, gently. Just having the cold brass of the knob in his hand made him feel as if he had already done something wrong. The knob turned fractionally before meeting a resistance. He went around the side of the house, past the garage, to a door he assumed led to a mudroom. The outer portion of this door swung open freely. In fact, there was no mechanism there to keep it closed. An inner door was more firmly shut, but there was no deadbolt. He took a magnetic card from his wallet, the one that admitted him to the hospital garage, and slid it into the door, just as he had seen it done in the movies. He entered the house.

Peter paused a moment in the hallway that led to the open part of the main floor to let his eyes adjust to the faint streetlight that suffused this part of the house. It was a vague light. It made all the objects around him seem composed of each other. There was no colour here. He could hear his heart in his neck, but otherwise, all was silent. After a few moments, the staircase to the second floor emerged out of the greyness, and he began to go up. The wooden banister under his hand was cool.

As he came toward the upper hallway, he began to hear the sounds of a sleeping household. To his right, and through a slightly open door, a man snored quietly. In the pauses between inhales, he could hear another's breathing, a sibilant but hollow sound that was almost exactly like Margot's breathing when she was asleep. Softer breathing came from the left. He continued down the hall. There were five more doors. One was open: a bathroom. Another was a narrow door, a closet of some kind. The other three were bedrooms.

He pushed the first door open. It slid against carpet. A crib, above which a mobile hung, stood out in silhouette against the back wall. A nightlight, plugged into the wall beneath the crib, projected the bars of the crib across the ceiling. The baby was sleeping on its stomach and had its head tucked, like a swan, into the warmth of its own body. He stepped away and closed the door. When his own children had been that small, such stillness and peacefulness seemed a signal to him that he and Margot were doing everything right. No child sleeps so soundly if it knows hunger or fear. This faceless infant was well loved, he thought. It did not yet know what kinds of people it lived with and that they could attract darkness.

The second door was the older boy's room. A pennant bearing the name of the baseball team Eric played on was on the door. *Pythons*, it said. Maybe the boy even played with Eric, although he was likely to be on another squad, a boy Eric perhaps looked up to. Peter put the flat of his palm on the door and pushed it open, and the faint light from the hall seeped in, illuminating the bed and the body in it. He stepped into the verge, cutting the light out, and waited for his eyes to adjust. It smelled like Eric's room, a boyish smell cut with an edge of sourness. Peter could put his face in Eric's hair and smell the milky warmth of his scalp. Eric's lanky body was covered in a blond down, and he was shy of it. He was harmless. All he cared about was his video games and making his mother laugh. Peter thought, if he could, he would freeze him at this age, while he was still a delight.

But the smell in the room was also his smell. He recognized that he had brought his own funk along. He wondered why humans' instincts were so in abeyance that they could not smell a threat in their own burrow. He had not awakened to the threat in his household, in the body of his daughter. He'd been oblivious to it; it had moved through the rooms of his life like something familiar.

Peter stepped into the room. There was a bat on the floor—he touched it with the tip of a shoe and rolled it toward himself, and then pushed it silently under the bed. His eyes had adjusted and he could see the boy's face now, in profile against his pillow. He recognized the spiky blond hair over the forehead. He saw it in his mind's eye, bent down against the small of his daughter's back, her face buried in the boy's groin, the boy's eyes closed, as now, only more conscious, the lids clenching and unclenching. He knew, when he'd looked at the image, what the boy was feeling; there was no end to the alikenesses he'd sensed when he looked at that video. He'd even remembered, for the first time in many years, his earliest kiss. It was on a dare, in a closet, and the closet was as dark as the boy's room. The girl's name was Casey. She was small and limber; he recalled that she was a gymnast. Her mouth had tasted metallic. Someone shouted "Time!" outside the door, and they'd pulled away, and Peter had become immediately aware of the fact that his erection hurt. He was thirteen then. If they hadn't called time, if he'd been alone with her in there, would the urgency of the sensations in his body have compelled him to carry the encounter further? What if Casey had resisted him? What if she'd pushed him on?

His body felt cool in the comfortable dark of the boy's room, and except for the back of his neck, his skin was dry. He could see the outline of the boy's scapulae, the side of the multi-panelled cranium, the bone that was so fragile in babies that it was the one most frequently broken in newborns, the plates of the cranium sliding over the grey ocean below it.

The boy stirred in the bed, and Peter stilled himself. He heard him take a deep, waking breath, and the boy turned his head on the pillow, so that he was looking toward the foot of the bed. He called out quietly. He was seeing his father in the doorway, in the gloom. He got no answer and raised himself on one elbow and squinted out into the dark. Peter could see his face clearly now, there was no doubt in his mind, he would not be punishing the wrong person. The boy looked confused, and stayed silent, not certain of where he was, or even if he was dreaming.

"Go back to sleep," Peter said. He made no effort to disguise his voice. The stillness between himself and the boy drew out and neither of them moved. "Go back to sleep."

The boy let himself back down onto the pillow and pulled his covers about himself. In a matter of a few seconds, his breathing slowed down again, deep dreaming breaths, the boy's mind sliding to another place. Peter watched him.

ORCHARDS

This is a little story that sometimes one of my sons asks me
to tell. It's about a day in January when I was ten, when
my little brother and I found a dead dog in the middle of
the road. We'd just come out of Harrison Road and onto
York Mills where it starts its long slow dip toward the
intersection at Bayview Avenue. Adam—who's of course
an uncle now, imagine—had his skates draped over his
neck, the cold iron blades knocking up against each other,
while I had mine in my bag. We each carried our own
Stan Mikita stick. When the light changed, we crossed
and headed down the hill toward the arena. It was very
cold and getting dark, and the cars had their lights on. The
ones heading in the direction of the traffic lights below
were curving around a spot part-way down, and when we
got there, we saw a big black newf lying there that had
probably walked into traffic and been hit by a car coming
over the hill. Other cars had nudged the dog lower, so it
came to rest in the middle of the incline. The animal lay
on its side, its nose pointing straight across the road, one
yellow line disappearing under its back and another
coming out under its belly. It looked like it had been
struck by a cartoon arrow.

We knew dogs—we'd watched our father whelp pups
in the basement of our house, in a little kennel made of

plywood he'd knocked together for them. We'd seen them being born. They came out in shiny grey sacs, already struggling, and if the mother (our dog, Sam—we don't have dogs now, allergies) didn't free them with her teeth, our father carefully slit the sacs with a penknife, and they'd gush out, wet and keening, their eyes closed. For weeks, the basement smelled of blood and fur, and Adam and I would go down after supper and look at the eight pups blindly snuffling their mother. Sam was a Bernese Mountain Dog, and when we were smaller, we rode her around the yard. She once dragged Adam out of the ravine at the back, pulling him by the neck of his T-shirt and growling at him the whole time. Our father called Sam "Mother," since she was so protective of us and our real mother had died when Adam was a baby. If you were ever in our house at a certain time of day, you'd hear Dad say, "Leonard, go feed your mother," and someone would have to explain to you that that was what he called the dog.

But when she had the pups, Sam changed. If Adam or I picked one of them up, she'd lift her head and watch us carefully and if the pup made a frightened noise, Sam would draw her lips back over her black and pink gums and she'd even show a long white tooth, although she never snapped or even made a sound.

Adam didn't know our mother, although he could identify her in pictures. Everyone on the street knew our father was raising us by himself—this was the 1970s, keep in mind—and the thing he cared most about was that we looked okay in our clothes and didn't go out without hats and gloves in the winter. There was a park near the house that we went to almost every day, and he seemed to know a lot of people there, especially women, and sometimes he'd ask me how I'd feel if he got married again. I always told him that would be fine with me, but I didn't want anyone who had boy children because Adam was enough, and we could probably use an older sister. He'd joke with me, saying that he'd made a deal with one of the women in the park and that he was going to trade me for a car or for a player "to be named later." Funny guy, I'd tell him. Other times he'd warn me or Adam to behave or he'd send us down to the farm team. I know what he meant now, but then I thought it was really a farm and I was curious and then disappointed that my behaviour was never bad enough to get me sent there.

But the story. We were on York Mills, and Adam held his stick out and walked into the road. It was icy and some of the cars that went around him fishtailed as they passed. I followed him into the stream of traffic and the two of us went and stood by the dead animal. There was no blood, no mark on the dog; it was as if it had wandered out into the street and died there of natural causes. Adam knelt down beside the body and stroked its cold fur. The cars made a parenthesis of motion around us. We got a hold of the dog's front legs and tugged it so it pointed nose-forward down the hill. The big Silverdale 115 bus came over the hill and whined down past us. Then we got behind the dog and used our Stan Mikitas to move it off to the side of the road. It was hard work. The dog kept slipping the wrong way, sliding from our sticks and slowly careering down the hill instead of toward the curb. Adam hit the road with his stick in a rage whenever the big body refused to cooperate. The cars honked and passed closely and some of the drivers called out to us, but we didn't answer. We could have been killed.

We'd got all our hockey equipment from Mrs. Mendel, who lived two doors up from us. She was lonely all the time and told Adam and me to come over for cookies whenever we wanted. Nell, the girl who lived across the road, told me that one day Mrs. Mendel found her son asleep in the car inside the garage. I didn't know this meant he was dead, but I think on some level I knew he must have been, and this was why she was lonely. When Adam and I went to visit her, we'd walk across the two backyards that separated us from her house, walking along the bulrushes that lined the edge of the ravine. Next to us were the Goldmans, and then it was the Ponnusamys, whose cooking smelled interesting. Mrs. Mendel lived alone, although her basement was full of hockey equipment that was only there for me and Adam. She was the one who gave us our first skates, and when our father tried to return them she told him he was being proud. We had a special knock that we'd use on the side door, and then she'd let us in and pour us each a glass of milk and give us two Coffee Break cookies. She wouldn't eat with us, but sit at the table and ask us questions, like what our bedtimes were, and who were our friends at school. Then when we were finished, she'd open the door to the basement and let us go down to play, telling us to let ourselves out the side door when we were ready to go. I'd take Adam's hand and bring him home in the dark.

This street, which we lived on our whole childhoods, had once been part of an orchard. Our father was good at knowing about the history of places. The orchard had been owned by a man who also raised horses and our dad told us that sometimes when people dug out their basements in the area, they found horse bones. There was only one tree left from the orchard and it never flowered anymore. I had Boy Scout meetings up at Harrison Road Public School, and I had to pass it on Wednesday nights. The tree was lit up under the streetlamps, gnarled and silent like the black trees in the forest of *Snow White*. This is my earliest memory of being frightened of the dark, because when I passed the tree, I thought it could do anything to me it wanted. So I'd talk to it. I'd stop in front of it, in the dark, and greet it and tell it where I'd been and then wish it a good night. I believed for some time that I survived my childhood only because I supplicated this old tree.

When Adam and I got the dog to the curb we had to stop because we couldn't lift it over and onto the verge. I told Adam to go back out into the street and wave his stick until someone pulled over. Someone finally stopped, and we were both surprised to see that it was Mrs. Mendel. She rushed around the front of her car and slapped me hard on the cheek and then picked Adam up and held him in her arms. But she didn't hurry him off the road; she held him against her, the headlights of the cars behind her casting a huge shadow down the hill. I was worried that she was going to do something to him, but I was also frightened to go near her again. Finally, she came over to the curb and sat down, folding her body over Adam, and she was crying. I shook her sleeve and she lifted her face to me and let him go. He came and stood beside me. Then she put us in the back seat of her car and drove us home in complete silence.

I recall Adam slipping his hand across the seat to hold mine and that it had become fully dark by then. Lights were on in all the houses we passed driving back along Harrison Road toward our street. It started to snow and Adam leaned across the seat and whispered to me, *this will make it harder for people to see the dog.* I can see it so clearly, the snow drifting down onto the road and into the trees, the snow against the sky, dark clusters that glowed star-white when they passed through Mrs. Mendel's headbeams.

Imagine your father trying to shove a dead dog to the side of the road in the middle of winter with nothing but a hockey stick. My sons laugh when they imagine me as a boy, doing this. What they don't know, and what I don't tell them, is that this is probably the only day I remember from that year, a single day left standing from an orchard of days. So they laugh, although they understand it's a warning about something, this remembrance, this little story.

A LARK

It was the most common of love sicknesses. Bergman, at the brink of forty, had fallen in love with a girl. There was no excuse for his behaviour—he was contentedly, if not ecstatically, married, and his work was stable and sometimes even interesting. All of this made his longing for Claudia as incomprehensible (he was a "good" man) as it was or seemed to be unstoppable. He had spent a month in Calgary on assignment, setting up a switching hub in a suburb that had grown by three hundred per cent in four years. His was an office job, keeping track of the work, keeping his crews on schedule. There were new papers every morning for him to look through and approve, and they were neatly threaded onto a large ring binder. Bright white sheets with rows and columns demonstrated the slow spread of a new network through which the settlers of this greenest new edge of suburbia would now be able to communicate with each other and the rest of the world. He had gone into the field once, but it had been more to show support of his crews than to inspect them. The boom in information technology had seen to it that a company as large as his could hire the most capable engineers, technicians, and fieldworkers, and he knew that exactly the right measures were being taken, and at a pace that was acceptable to everyone. And so, Bergman was deemed good at his job by the men in Toronto who had sent him to Calgary, and by everyone who had become his temporary co-worker there.

Claudia was at the company as a trainee. She was twenty-four, and fresh out of a small west coast managerial college. He had fallen in with her quite naturally, forgetting who and what he was since his true milieu was not around to reflect this back at him. He winningly parodied the marital stumblings and failings that were the commonplaces of midlife, convincingly enough that she didn't think he would be susceptible to such foolishness. He didn't look quite as old as thirty-eight and had a pleasing fringe of grey hair behind his temples that was sparse enough to give him some character without rendering him fatherlike. He'd kept his shape as well, even though he had thickened, but it happened in the way (so he liked to think) that it had happened to Mel Gibson, which is to say an agreement had been struck with gravity that was valid as long as his body fat did not go up over fifteen per cent.

Bergman was the first "grown" man Claudia had ever met who was not hardwired to the adult circuit board that her own parents came from. He was from somewhere else, towing some scent of his life behind him, but essentially apart from it in this foreign place, some bit of fifth business detached from the background.

He had, naturally, noticed her right away. He noticed women as a matter of course, and had an ongoing monologue in his mind about them, stating without affect some quality that struck him: *what fantastic hair, eyes like a doe.* When he'd first seen Claudia, she was wearing a pair of riding chaps (the kind intended for fashion, rather than for horses) and he thought, *Grace Kelly rides again.* As a rule, Claudia dressed more brightly than the other women in the office, and had a clear, liquid laugh that could be heard anywhere on the floor. She was tall in the way of thin, small-breasted girls, *willowy*, a certain kind of book would have called her, even though she was of average height. There was a sharpness about her that was expressed especially in her arms and legs, and the skin on the backs of her hands seemed tightly wrapped, showing the grain of her sinews. She appeared intensely delicate to Bergman, and this made him want to run a fingertip down her body, lightly.

What had started with fast-food meals progressed to drinks (in order to "continue talking"), and from there they could both feel what was happening, and it was like being perched at the top of the first hill on a roller coaster. Bergman had a room at the Radisson, where they'd gone one June night after a couple of extra drinks. She'd allowed him to slide her long, red linen dress off her shoulders and to the floor, where it pooled in ripples around her feet as if she were a pink stone thrown into a deep red pond. She did not wear a bra, there were no lines on her chest or back where one had just been removed, and it struck Bergman that under her dress she was like a sculpture of a woman. She slipped a finger into the band of her panties and drew one leg up and out. Just two pieces of clothing on her, imagine. They had sex in the giant hotel bed, and in the middle of her dove-cries, her chest flushing red above him, Bergman thought he had gone too far. But then Claudia folded herself down onto him, and the smell of her hair and the sensation of her damp arms convinced him that he was doing what he ought to, if only he viewed what was happening from a certain perspective, and that perspective included the reality of the briefness of life, and the idea that remaining open to new experiences was a positive thing.

He was telling the traditional lies to all involved. To his wife, Renata, the work was going slowly, and there was little in the way of entertainment where he was. Just a neighbourhood video store that stocked all the films they'd seen together earlier in the year, and a local bar where he (*daringly*, he described it) allowed himself the occasional pint of beer and conversation with the barkeep. He'd ventured to participate in a game of darts with some men from his crew whom he'd happened upon, and he'd deepened his bonds. That there was no local, and therefore no dart board or crewmen to be played with, gave the story dimensions that Bergman thought were closer to engineering than mere lying.

"Will the contract end on time?" Renata asked him.

"I hope so," said Bergman. "I don't want to miss the fall in the city."

"No, dear," she said, and blew him a kiss down the line.

★

On most nights after work, Claudia would collect him from a spot a few streets away from the company's offices and they'd walk to her car and then drive to downtown. She favoured Japanese food and steak, and so they'd usually eat in a good restaurant on the company card and then walk hand-in-hand (an open transgression that made him feel invulnerable) down the mall in the middle of the city, the spiky tower looming over them. He'd been to Calgary once as a boy to watch the rodeo and, with the Instamatic camera his father had given him as a birthday present, he'd photographed the fireworks that came afterward. When the photos came back, they were black as pitch. Now, as an adult, he couldn't even remember what the rodeo or the fireworks had been like.

"I'm not frightened to hold your hand," he told her. "Although I want you to know I've never done this before."

"Held a girl's hand?" They were still bantering like this even though they'd already been intimate. He took it as an indication that she was enjoying spending any kind of time with him, and it made him feel expansive, like there was considerable substance to him that had been packed away over the years of his marriage that anyone who took the time could have to herself. It was nice to air himself out.

"You know that's not what I mean," he said. "I mean I'm not prone to misbehaving."

She puckered. "That makes me feel like I'm being bad."

"Oh no," he said, "you're not. Well, a little. Maybe

you'll have to go to bed early as punishment."

His feeble flirting didn't get a smile. He'd noticed these little clouds going past and he'd already learned that changing the subject—or simply not following up on it— was as effective as trying to find out what was going on inside her head. He swung her arm a little and she pulled it still and drew the length of herself up against him. "Buy me an ice cream," she said.

"Still hungry?"

"I have the metabolism of a bird."

"A hummingbird!"

"Yes, I'm a hummingbird. And you're a lark."

He laughed. But later, when he thought about it, he wondered if she had said something significant, if she was saying to him that he was a hobby, or perhaps the reverse: that she was just a little diversion to him. It pained him and he lay awake beside her and replayed the comment in his mind. *If I am a lark, then she is just having fun at my expense. But if she thinks I'm larking, then she thinks I could hurt her.* He woke her after an hour of this and asked her what she meant. She blinked at him in the dull light of the hotel room.

"What I meant by what?"

"The lark thing. Do you think I'm not serious?"

"Have you never seen a lark? They're larger than hummingbirds and more confident. That's all I meant. You're a poor city boy, aren't you?"

"No, I just thought you were trying to tell me something."

She lay back down and tilted her head at him on the pillow, then made a faint cheeping noise. "You've robbed the nest, lark. You've been very bad."

"Stop it. I was worried."

"Why worry?" she said, and she closed her eyes.

He tried to sleep. But he was kept awake by the thought that what he'd really wanted was to feel as if what they were doing mattered to her, if only to satisfy himself that she was involved. Emotionally, he told himself.

For another couple of weeks, the work continued apace, even though when Bergman riffled through the morning reports and the numbers (which translated into hubs and switching stations and wires and houses) they now seemed a little less transparent to him and more like a code. Perhaps, he realized, he was hoping a mistake or two would slip by and force an extension in his stay. He spoke distractedly of progress whenever he was consulted by head office. Sometimes he sat at the gleaming black meeting-room table with a number of his colleagues and spoke into a conferencing camera about signal strengths and NAS lines and subscribers. On the television screen, which was usually propped at the end of the table, a disembodied head listened and nodded sometimes and spoke to people off-camera on its own end. Invariably, it all ended with an encouragement to continue the excellent work.

And Claudia was doing well in the eyes of their superiors, and there was some talk of making a position for her somewhere else in the country. She reassured him that the relocation would take months, that there was no need to think of it now. So he didn't, and they continued their affair as if it were untouched by concerns of the external world. When they were together there was no company and no work. It had reached the point that neither of them knew the status of the other's project anymore. He didn't realize that their love affair had put her somewhat behind; he had risen far enough that the managerial competence he demonstrated almost obviated work for him, whereas she was still learning. And now floundering a little. One weekend evening, she had even borrowed a spare key-card to gain access to the office so that she could finish a report. She came back though, in the early dawn hours, and to his delight had woken him with her mouth.

He began to share his age-old stories with her. The calcified tales of childhood (army bases, drowned brother, hockey), then his adolescence, and up to the middle of his twenties. It amazed him to see his early life rebloom after so many years of never having the need to speak of it. The richness of those years, and the sheer amount of experience in them, made him feel as if the earlier parts of his life had been compacted for storage. It had been so long since he'd been more than his daily life. He recalled his earliest experiences with women, the clumsy carnality, and he made her laugh, playing this older, life-scarred man, depicting his younger self as an inept lover, a bumbler. But he stopped before his marriage. He did not want to speak about Renata.

"You can talk about your wife, you know," she'd said. "I won't be jealous."

"I'm not sure you'd have a right to be."

"I'm just saying, I can take it. It's all a part of you."

She was democratic in this, as in most things. A function of not being old enough to know what could hurt her. And so he told her how he and Renata had met, sanding down some of the more loving details, making it sound like it was a low-grade passion that had brought them together, and mostly pleasing, if bland, ritual that sustained them. (As he said all of this, he realized that it was not true, not even remotely. He thrived on routine, and whenever he was away from home for any length of time he craved it and he craved Renata. It was possible, it came to him, to be perfectly content in a marriage and still be capable of infidelity, and this surprised him. It meant that a person's feelings could develop along parallel tracks. He thought, as he was talking to Claudia about Renata, that he actually still loved Renata, but that the *still loved* was a false kind of continuance; there was no need to presume he would have stopped. He was buoyed by this thought.)

He told Claudia of the houses bought and sold, the failed attempt at adoption, the death of his mother, and then Renata's. Claudia nodded through it all, but he saw that, despite her brave reassurances, it was too much for her. It wasn't the fact of Renata that was bothering her, he realized, but the fact of history. There was a great deal of it.

"You've been through a lot together," she said.

"We've been married for some time."

"In the olden days," she said, "men had wives *and* mistresses. But the mistresses were always alone when they got old. Discarded."

"I won't discard you," he said, and he felt he meant it. He noticed that her eyes were wet now. "I'm sorry. I didn't mean to hurt you."

She shrugged and then touched the corner of her eye and sucked the tip of her finger. He leaned over and kissed the other eye, tasted the trace of salt there. She lowered herself into his lap and sighed theatrically, then laughed. "I'm being dramatic," she said, but she didn't sit up and he saw her ribs shaking. Some whole other part of her was suddenly present then, and he did not know what to say or do. He rubbed her side and her back, and in comforting her he felt frightened. Here was a woman silently weeping in his lap! *Because* of him. A strange comparison rose to mind, and he recalled himself, just the previous night, holding Claudia's hips tight to his own, not allowing her to move, and she'd come with a cry of astonishment. That seemed a much more complicated physiological reaction to set in motion than making someone weep, but now the weeping seemed immensely personal, much more personal than being inside someone's body. He gripped Claudia by the shoulders and lifted her up and told her he would drive her home. "I'm fine," she said, and indeed she had collected herself. Another cloud passing.

"No," said Bergman. "I think we need an evening apart."

"Because I cried a little? Come on now." She sniffed once and looked at him with dark eyes. "Girls like to cry sometimes. It's cleansing. Let's go for our walk."

"We can walk tomorrow," he said.

She straightened herself. "You know what? You promised to buy me a cowboy hat. You can't take me home. You have to buy me a hat and bring me back to the hotel and see what I look like with it on."

He immediately pictured her cavorting in nothing but the cowboy hat, her long black hair tucked up underneath it so she looked like a cascade of bright skin. It moved him to pull her to her feet and take her down to one of the stores, where he bought her a Stetson as close to her skin colour as he could find. As if programmed to draw her close even as he'd been trying to push her away. Back in the hotel room, shaking, he tucked her hair under the hat, and undressed her, and she stood at the foot of the bed, one hip cocked, pretending to shoot him and then blew smoke away from her finger. After they made love, he insisted on driving her home, and she sat in the passenger seat of his rented car with her bottom lip sucked into her mouth.

"I have work to do," he told her.

"That's okay." She was determined to sound as if there was nothing wrong. She got out of the car and doffed her hat to him. A good sport.

Back at the hotel, where Bergman had no work, he

stood at the window that overlooked the western end of the city and followed the main road with his eye until it reached the scrubby edge of town and then flattened out before it rose up into the mountains. He realized that if he was not, by definition, a bad man, then he probably wasn't a good one, either. His mind felt gluey. He had not called his wife in many days. When he dialled the number, she answered sleepily and asked him to call again the next day. He wanted badly to keep her on the line and talk to her— amazing, he thought, that he would reach out to her at a time like this. *What am I doing*, he thought. He told his wife he loved her and she sleepily said she loved him and they hung up.

Bergman made himself difficult to reach at work. He crumpled up the sticky notes that Claudia left on his divider, and involved himself in intricate, sometimes imaginary conversations on the phone when he heard her voice or her laugh on the floor, or saw her coming his way. A few days after he'd bought her the cowboy hat, she stopped his elevator and got in with him. "I won't be hurt if you want to end this, but you could say something."

"I think I do want to end it," he said, surprising himself. "I feel like I'm doing something wrong."

"I thought that's what you liked about it. That someone would let you behave like this."

The doors opened and they walked out silently. He realized immediately that he had lied to her about wanting to end it, but it made him feel noble. Doing the right thing. She walked away toward the revolving doors. It was getting harder to determine what was cowardice. That he had taken up with a young girl and told himself that he loved her? Or that now, pushing her away from him, he was turning away from life? Yes, it was wrong to do what he had done, but in listening (so it seemed) to these imperatives, had he not determined to stay fastened to the force that until very recently appeared to drive him and every other bit of nature as well? He watched her cross the sun-bright parking lot, waving and smiling at a co-worker about her age, a man named Davis, whose wife Bergman had met. The two of them out there seemed co-conspirators in something he once knew the rules of. He had pushed her away because it felt, for a moment, that he was ruining them both and participating in an act so dishonourable that he would never be forgiven for it. Now he regretted it. For the rest of the afternoon, he bearded himself. *You are a fool. You did treat this as a lark, didn't you?*

That night, the conversation with Renata did not go well. It was as if they had both forgotten their roles. She did not ask him about the pain in his hand that was one of his general conditions. He'd called the previous night, forgetting that Wednesday evenings she volunteered at the local community centre and refereed the girls' indoor soccer league, and so had also forgotten she most often went to bed early on Wednesdays. He had been gone most of two months now, and his body had adjusted to

Claudia's: his mouth to hers, his pelvis to hers, her back to his chest. But also, he saw, his rhythms to hers: their way of speaking. So he cut off his wife continually in their conversation, pausing to ask her to *go on*, and then waiting until he was sure he could speak without interrupting. He manufactured more stories of the local pub, something about an outdoor league that he realized was triggered by the soccer games Renata had officiated. There wasn't much of him now that wasn't completely made up. He told her about an imaginary meeting in the morning that was to start early, and she read him as he'd intended: "Go to bed now, then," she said. "We'll talk again on the weekend."

The next day, he got in to work resolved that his momentary loss of faith in the elevator would be corrected, and he went immediately to Claudia's cubicle. She was writing quietly behind her desk and cast an anxious glance first toward him and then at the woman in the cubicle immediately beside her. He gestured with his head toward the supply room, and they went in and shut the door. Right away, he put his hands behind her neck and drew her in to kiss her, but she went stiff and pulled away.

"You can't drop me one day and then have me the next!"

"That was wrong, what I said to you yesterday. I'm in love with you."

Her face screwed up in horror. "No you're not! You're not at all."

"I am, Claudia. I was just beside myself yesterday after we spoke. I felt awful. It's because . . . my emotions—"

"Your emotions *what*?" she said, and stared at him with her hands on her hips. After a silent moment she looked up toward the ceiling as if she couldn't stand to witness his confusion any longer. "Fucking hell," she muttered, and she put her hands on his shoulders and drove him down into a chair. "You don't love me, you just want me," she said. "It's not good enough that I'll sleep with you and listen to your stories and spend all my time with you. You want some part of me that you can really hurt so it feels *real* to you."

"What are you talking about?"

"Do you think I'm in love with *you*? Have you thought about that at all?"

"Look, I'm trying to tell you how I feel," he said, bewildered, but with that, she turned and pulled open the door, leaving him sitting there in the tiny room.

The next morning, Claudia's desk was cleared and her cubicle empty. Panicked, Bergman went around her floor asking after her in as casual a voice as he could muster, but no one seemed to know where she was. He tried her cell, but she didn't answer, and instead of the personal message she'd recorded, an operator's voice (he'd actually met this woman, she worked for the company as well) said *the party you have dialled is not available*. For a few days, he chalked up her absence to a cubicle change that was no doubt connected to their run-in in the supply room. The company had three buildings in the city, and she could have plausibly requested a change of scenery to help her develop her grasp of the firm's workings. She could have cleverly arranged the move with no questions asked. But at the beginning of the next week (after a harrowing weekend in which he and Renata had argued about retiling the master bathroom, and he had wandered in the vicinity of each of the company's offices, thinking perhaps he would find Claudia), he went to her supervisor and told her he needed to contact Claudia, wherever she was. The woman, Mrs. Farrell, folded her hands under her chin and regarded him.

"Why do you need to contact Ms. Jordan?"

He hadn't considered his reason, and then recalled the entry card. Yes, he'd lent it to her, and forgotten about it. "I think she may have one of my key-cards," he said.

"Why does she have one of your key-cards, Mr. Bergman? What happened to hers?"

"I don't think she had one yet. She wanted to do some work on the weekend, so she asked me to borrow mine." He drew back a chair and sat down, giving himself a moment to think. "She's very keen on succeeding with the company."

"Were you entirely proper?" asked Mrs. Farrell.

"Was I—?"

"She was not entitled to a card of her own, so why would you think she should be carrying yours?"

"It's my fault, definitely," said Bergman. "I should have seen her into the building myself, but I didn't think there'd be any harm in it. And of course, I had no idea she'd be leaving."

"Well, Ms. Jordan was transferred to the field. She's in Yellowknife, at least for now."

"Oh. Well, that's great," said Bergman. "How can I reach her, then?"

"No need for a long-distance call," said Mrs. Farrell. "I don't imagine Ms. Jordan will be able to put your card to any bad use where she is right now."

He left the office offering a smile of thanks.

His ill-considered story had repercussions. Within the day, Mrs. Farrell summoned Bergman back to her office. She'd called the Yellowknife operation and spoken to Claudia to see how she was doing. In passing she had mentioned that Bergman had inquired after his key-card, and Claudia had denied borrowing it. Mrs. Farrell pressed her, reminding her that an employee of Mr. Bergman's long standing would not have a reason to lie about such a thing, and that she, Claudia, was not in any trouble. "But," said Mrs. Farrell to him, "you know how once you tell a lie, no matter how insignificant, it's pride to some people to stick to it regardless the consequences. Do you know what I mean?"

"Yes," he said in a quiet voice. He imagined that Claudia had weighed the situation. The company was looking for his entry card, and perhaps he was in some trouble. If the affair were found out, and the card made a tangible link between them, then perhaps it would be proved that he had fraternized with someone at least ostensibly under him and he would be fired. So she was protecting him. Or maybe in denying that she had the card, she was trying to flush him out into the open. But it was clear, if she had tried to impugn him, that she had not succeeded.

Mrs. Farrell looked very stern, and she still had one hand on the phone, where, he imagined, she had cut off Claudia's voice just before he entered.

"You were just trying to be a good colleague."

"Yes," he said, his hands and feet beginning to tingle.

"Well, it's best to know these things about people before they get too entangled in the company."

"I suppose."

She took her hand off the phone and looked down at her papers. His chest felt like someone was pressing on it. "And Mr. Bergman?"

"Yes."

"The company card is not a free-for-all." He wondered for a moment if she thought he lent his key-cards to everyone. "Pay for some of your own dinners, please."

"I will," said Bergman, with some relief, and then turned to leave. From the doorway, he said, "You told her I had come to you?"

"Of course I did."

"What did she say?"

"What do you mean? She made her bed."

"Yes. Thank you," said Bergman, and he went back to his cubicle as if in a dream. A spreadsheet was on the screen, a tightly ordered array of cells in rows and columns that flooded the edges of the display. Then, as he was staring at it, the program blinked out and the screen went dark and the computer expressed a bright green tube that swept up to the top of the screen, and then came back down, receding into the darkness of the false perspective and back out. He imagined himself entangled in the snaking forms. When he touched the keyboard, the patterns disappeared and the spreadsheet popped back into view. For the first time in weeks, he tried to focus his mind, and he did some proper work. He tried to figure out the amount of time the remainder of the project would take. He read his e-mails and assembled a checklist of items that had been brought to his attention—some weak links and unfinished tests. He e-mailed the foreman this list and then the phone rang and it was the very same man, laughing, telling him it had already been done. He wanted to know if Bergman would join them for a beer, but Bergman said it wouldn't be possible.

What became especially difficult was that none of what he had done seemed to have the power to come back to him. He had his misgivings after the run-in with Mrs. Farrell, but in a matter of days, he stopped feeling bad about it.

In the last week of his assignment, he was not once accosted by anyone who had twigged to the terrible things his idle plotting had wrought. His co-workers and his crewmen treated him with respect, shared their jokes with him, and began reminiscing about the intense two months it had taken to bring this job to completion. A sense of common accomplishment filled the office, and he was brought into its warmth and accorded credit.

Mrs. Farrell said goodbye to him on his last day, shaking his hand and telling him she was sure they'd meet again, but hopefully somewhere with better restaurants. It was as if neither he nor Mrs. Farrell had been connected to Claudia in even the most peripheral of ways. Later that morning, he noticed some of the cubicle offices were being dismantled, and for the first time he realized that these offices didn't permanently belong to the company. They set up office simulacra wherever they needed to and then pulled them down. It wasn't an uncommon thing to do, but he'd arrived after the project had started and had never realized that he'd been on a kind of set. Next week it would belong to a theatre festival, and maybe after that, to a political campaign. All evidence of his work here, and the site of his love affair, was to be taken apart and reassembled for the pageant of some other set of histories. He shook hands with his office-mates, some of whom had chipped in to buy him a fine pen as a goodbye gift. They had liked him, and he hadn't noticed.

On his last afternoon, he walked slowly along the mall where he had bought Claudia her hat, and wondered if she had gone home from Yellowknife. He hoped that somehow she had come back to Calgary and that he would run into her and explain how what had happened had happened. But the streets were quiet in the afternoon, and the hat store was closed—for a family funeral, said a sign in the door. *At least she would never have second thoughts now*, he told himself. *At least she is free of me*. He allowed himself to imagine a series of worse outcomes. That they *had* been caught. That he had left his wife. That Claudia had rejected him.

Yet none of these things seemed remotely possible, and not just because they hadn't happened, but because what he'd done had had no consequences.

Bergman returned to the city where he lived with his wife, and that summer they carried on with the rituals they had established among their friends, having barbecues and playing golf. During the time he'd been away, Renata had slimmed down a little, and this he imagined had been done for him, although she told him at one point that she felt better and liked fitting into some of her old clothes.

It was a bright, temperate summer. His tomatoes did well, and some mornings, looking out the window, the world he lived in seemed hallowed. At times, when he and Renata argued, as they did in their way (he never thought of it as anything more than one of the benign commonplaces of marriage), he would think of telling her what he'd done. It would happen during a silence—as she was looking at him, her head tilted, waiting for an answer to something. In those few moments, suspended between responding to what was at hand and revealing what she did not suspect, Bergman felt that he could bend the entire future in his hands. Just a word, and everything would change. Two years earlier, he'd taken a phone call from Renata's father and learned that Renata's mother had passed away. Bergman walked toward the den where his wife was reading. Her father was waiting on the line. But she didn't see Bergman standing back from the doorway in the hall and as he watched her, he thought, *She is still in the old life*. He could wait silently and give her a few more moments in a time and place where her mother was still living. He stood there for what seemed like many minutes, watching her so peacefully, so happily involved in her book.

He never told her about Claudia. The summer ended. In the fall, work became busier, as it usually did, with new services being introduced and the expansion of existing ones into the burgeoning suburbs of various cities. Bergman had done his tour of duty, however, and other mid-management personnel were sent to Edmonton, to Halifax, to Ottawa. He stayed in the home office, in his true office, the one with the pictures and the diplomas. He'd chosen the carpet in that office, with an allowance the company had given him. He returned to his usual lunch places and ate with the usual group of co-workers.

Bergman still thought about Claudia, but mostly to go over in his mind the story he'd constructed for her life after Calgary. She had bounced back. She worked for another company, a strong, young competitor on the west coast that would give her more than the old company ever would have. She was meeting new people. There was a man, her age, who found the richness of her spirit and body a marvellous bewilderment. As work became more consuming, he found that he thought of her less and less. He picked the last of his tomatoes. The leaves fell.

As they did most autumns, he and Renata took a weekend and drove into the States, looking at the changing colours down through the Finger Lakes. They spent an evening in a colonial inn, near a dry riverbed, and walked among the identical stones of the revolutionary dead that rose on a hill beside the stone inn. That night, the inn's restaurant made a mistake on another couple's dinner reservation, and there was no room for them. Bergman gallantly offered them the other side of their tiny table.

They were from Amherst, upstate, and newly married. The man was probably in his mid to late twenties and he had the face of an altar boy. His bride was their age—a grown woman, as Renata would say. The couple sat down with words of thanks and tried to allow their "hosts" some privacy, but it was not possible. Renata, an excellent conversationalist, drew them in, and the four of them passed a pleasant two hours, talking of the history of that part of the country and their experiences in towns nearby. The woman collected antiques and shared with them a couple of choice locations off the beaten track. She modelled a ring that her new husband had bought her at one such store, old Irish silver.

Once they had started on their second bottle of wine (this was the most Bergman had drunk for many years), they relaxed thoroughly. They learned more about the other couple's histories—he was originally from Washington state, and she was an east coaster who had written a couple of books about Italian food. He and Renata told their own, well-rehearsed story, a happy one now that it was practised. Bergman asked how it was that the two of them, from opposite sides of the country, had found each other.

"It's a bit complicated," said the woman simply. "We met at the university."

"You met in a class?" said Renata

"No, no, not exactly." The couple shared a brief look. It made Bergman flinch. "It's a little embarassing," said the woman.

"That's all right," said Bergman. "Let's have another glass of wine."

The man held up his glass and Bergman poured, then filled the other glasses in turn. He felt suddenly displaced, and his movements were jerky. He was having a *déjà vu*, it felt. "I took Barbara's Italian class," the man said, bringing his wineglass away from his mouth. He looked over at his wife for a signal, and seemed to get one. "I guess we got a little too demonstrative with the transitive verbs."

They all laughed at this—it was done now, their transgression, and now it was between adults—and Barbara put her hand on her husband's and squeezed. Suddenly, a shape swam down into Bergman's mind, a whole flock of birds materializing above a wire and settling onto it. He'd never seen this woman before, but he felt he knew her, as if she were from his future, and had arrived here to show him where he was headed and what was waiting for him. And it was this: it was the company of the fallen. He was having a feeling, but it was also a form of knowledge, as if a series of words had been transformed into an electrical wave.

Renata put her hand on his arm and he flinched. "Honey?"

"Sorry," he said and he stood up as if stung, his chair squeaking along the parquet floor.

"Where are you going?"

He was in a restaurant, in New York state, with his wife and two strangers. He was going to turn forty in two weeks, and then the winter was going to come. "I'm making a toast," he said, and he turned himself back toward the table and reached for his wineglass. "Yes," he said, "to our new friends, on the occasion of our meeting."

"And to love," said the other husband, leaping up to join the gallantry. Both wives remained in their seats, watching their drunken husbands with affectionate looks. And after a moment waiting, the two men clinked their glasses and drank.

LOGIC OF REDUCTION

Josh, who isn't getting married in
September or December,
won't be marrying Evelyn.
—DELL LOGIC PUZZLES #78

Things went farther off in the wrong direction when
Robert said, "What do you think of getting married?" and
in order not to think about it Rebecca had got into the car
and come into town even though it was late at night and
almost everything was closed. The Rickshaw was open,
and so was the bar at The Arms, but Rebecca wasn't sure
if The Arms would have food. When she was a kid, there
always seemed to be faintly threatening men standing
around outside under the buzzing beer signs, and although
it was also a hotel, she'd never seen anyone come or go
with luggage.

The Rickshaw served Chinese and Canadian food, and
by Canadian the management meant pizza slices, ham-
burgers and fries, and all kinds of omelettes. Rebecca's
parents had once convinced her that french fries were
from China, but that, as with a lot of things (*gun powder,
noodles*), other people took credit for Chinese ingenuity.
They'd never gone into The Rickshaw, only made fun of
it when passing by on the way to their cottage, pointing

at the sign outside that showed a wooden cart being pulled by a boy. To be there now, drinking a cup of coffee and eating a very good piece of lemon pie, seemed a kind of rent in the fabric of her life. She lifted the cup to her mouth and the smell of the coffee calmed her nausea, but even so, sitting there alone and seemingly tranquil now, her pulse still sped up every few minutes, like coals touching off little spits of flame in a dead fire.

She'd left Kevin back at their friends' cottage, which was the opposite direction to where her family's place had been. She hadn't come this far north of Toronto in almost ten years, since they sold the old place and her father and mother split, and a lot of the things that seemed to have fit together for a long time came apart. It was strange to her, what began to feel "normal," but her parents living apart felt normal. Visiting them in their separate homes felt normal. Their individual tastes had come to the fore in such a way that the two homes seemed to represent an odd type of cell division. The silky lamps and deep velvety couches her mother favoured blossomed into a sort of Victorian den when left unchecked, while her father's apartment was a paradise of right-angled practicality: CD drawers that tilted out, tall thin lamps, a glass table supported by a hollow, wrought-iron box.

What didn't feel normal was *this* place, where the waitress hovered behind the counter, waiting for the night to end. It made Rebecca feel guilty to sit there, mulling things over, when everyone else was ready to go home.

★

Robert and Diane were Kevin's oldest friends, and a more established couple. Robert had been a senior partner in the firm that Kevin came to after completing his MBA; now, five years later, the two men were good friends. Rebecca was aware of a complex history between the three of them—she knew they'd seen Kevin through a difficult breakup—but Rebecca did not ask questions about a past she hadn't been a part of. During the year or so that she and Kevin had been together (they were about to buy a house, after a successful cohabitation since the end of the previous summer), they'd seen the other couple once or twice a month. Now, coming up to their cottage for the second time this summer, she could feel that she was on the verge of becoming a known quantity. She'd some time ago stopped feeling that she had to prove something to this older couple, but even as she relaxed more into their company, she also felt something being drawn tight around her.

The word was that Robert and Diane were failing, the marriage was breaking apart. They'd been together for more than ten years, and every time Rebecca had seen them they'd been as jolly as camp counsellors, finishing each other's sentences, telling stories in which the other had charmingly proved human in some way. Diane was colourful in the sense that Rebecca's mother would have meant it—i.e., weird—but Rebecca thought the older woman an interesting puzzle. She was unnaturally cheery, carrying on as if all the bruises life had to offer were just part of the fun. She suspected that Diane would be bright and bouncy in any situation. She might say, "Just nipping off to put a bullet in my head! Have another drinkie in the meantime!"

The more reserved of the two was Robert, but compared to either Rebecca or Kevin, he seemed almost as merry as his wife. Half of what he said made no sense to Rebecca, though—it was as if he spoke a parallel language that hived off into figures from some tongue Rebecca had never encountered. He once described Diane as being so drunk that "she was hanging off the wall and talking like a duck." The other two got him just fine, so Rebecca sometimes felt like a square in their company, party to a dialect she ought to have been able to decipher but couldn't. Her laughter was always catching up.

They'd reassured Kevin in private that everything was going to be okay with them. But as he drove north with Rebecca, Kevin told her it probably wouldn't be.

"Maybe they want to talk to us about it," she said.

"I doubt they want the advice of two people who still kiss in public."

"Maybe they're looking for inspiration."

"Let them bring it up, okay? I don't want to force them to talk about anything. Maybe they just need an injection of the old times." To Rebecca, their "old times" was a concoction she couldn't imagine the ingredients of, except that she was sure she wasn't in the recipe. In her experience, people always spoke swooningly of the old times, but they would rarely be willing to repeat their pasts. She was one of the people, so she thought, who *would* go back. To some of it, at least.

When Kevin and Rebecca arrived, their friends were waiting at the top of the driveway, and Diane broke into a trot down the little incline under the trees. Rebecca noticed she had to drop Robert's hand to start running. "Hello, hello!" she cried, her hair flying all over. She tore open Kevin's door and leaned in and kissed him even before he'd had a chance to turn the car off, and then she flung herself across his body to give Rebecca a hug. "Come!" she said. "My directions were good?"

"We've been here before," said Kevin. "Are you drunk already?"

Robert had arrived behind his wife. "You look delicious," he said to Rebecca.

Inside there were drinks already made. The ice in the bucket had fused into a big lump, as if they'd been expected earlier.

"You're meat, right?" Robert said to Rebecca.

"Sorry?"

"We're barbecuing the hell out of a giant slab of beef tonight. I just forget if that's okay with you.

"Oh, I'll eat anything," she said, and her mind went, *omni: everything, nulli: nothing.* "Whatever you're making is fine."

He went into the kitchen and opened the fridge, then stood back from the door making a game-show sweep with his hand. One shelf was burdened with the whole length of a piece of tenderloin, its silver sheath gleaming. They all applauded, and Robert took the big hunk of meat out of the fridge with his bare hands and held it upright so that he could make it bow to them. "You really like me!" he shrilled.

(She often thought her sense of disconnection from Robert might have come from an early experience she'd had with him. The first time she went up to their cottage, one morning just after sunrise, she left the little cabin that she and Kevin always slept in, to get a glass of juice, and found Robert standing naked in the big front window. He turned to her and asked her how she'd slept, then rubbed his hands together and got glasses down for both of them. Rebecca poured and tried to act normal as the two of them stood there drinking—she in her underwear and a T-shirt, Robert like some cumbersome animal not used to being upright, a bear trained to hold a glass. It wasn't the first time in her life she'd had to still a swirl of fear in herself, a fear that she had lost the horizon and didn't know where she was. He'd put his glass in the sink and padded back into his and Diane's bedroom, waving to her without turning around again. No doubt such an encounter had ripple effects, she thought.)

Robert barbecued the meal. There was the beef, and corn that had been soaked in water and then thrown on the grill in the husk, and oiled vegetables that he took care to turn so that they burned evenly on both sides. There was nothing going on the table that wasn't going to get barbecued. Maybe they'd grill breakfast, too.

She and Diane and Kevin stood nearby, Diane's back

against the railing. Rebecca was answering questions about work—she taught undergraduate English Literature—trying hard to make her personal experiences sound vital and interesting. She described her students as "eagerly terrified," but to her own ears, her phrases sounded flat. There was mainly the drip and sizzle of the meat, and the papery rattle of the cornhusks being turned. The air filled with stringy ash every time Robert touched them.

"How do you like her being surrounded by hard-bodied frat-boys there Kev?" asked Diane.

"No woman who knows her worth would want to go back to that," Kevin said. He put his arm around Rebecca and squeezed tight. "Why go back to beer when you've got wine?"

"Well, screw-cap wine," said Rebecca, but it came out not as funny as she'd intended, and she squeezed Kevin back to show she was joking. Robert flipped the piece of meat sideways, grunting like a weight-lifter making the snatch. It hit the grill with a muffled thud, a brutal sound to Rebecca's ears. The oiled flames jumped up and licked the underside. It felt to Rebecca as if the four of them had deserted a battle their fellows were still fighting and had come to a place of temporary respite, pretending everything was normal. She looked over at Diane, and the other woman suddenly seemed very far away, as if Rebecca were looking at her down the wrong end of a telescope. Her ears filled with a dullness she could hear her heartbeat through, and she detached herself from Kevin and put down her drink.

"Whoops," Kevin said.

"Too much on an empty stomach," said Rebecca. She turned her back and leaned against the railing beside Diane. If she breathed slowly, the feeling would pass.

Robert watched her with an analytical squint, a long silver fork in one hand, motionless over the grill, a steel spatula in the other. "Get the poor thing a little bunwich, Di," he said, pointing toward the door with the spatula, and Diane pushed herself off the railing and went inside. Rebecca felt the wood sway against her back.

Kevin put a solicitous hand on her shoulder. "You want to go in and rest a while?"

"Maybe I'll go down to the dock and sit in one of the chaises," she said.

Robert slapped the tenderloin with the flat of the spatula. "Bad Bessie!" he said. "You're turning our guests off." He looked up at Rebecca and smiled apologetically. "She'll bring you something. Go on down."

The last time Rebecca had been on her parents' lake, she was twenty-five. There had been a white dock lying on the water and a trail that led up to a wood-stained cottage in the pine. A short canoe ride away, there were two inlets that ended in marshes connected by a beaver dam. She'd been there many times, with her mother or father, or both, and sometimes she came alone and let the boat drift in the calm water. The summer home was the only place on earth that hadn't changed for her since she'd been a child. From time to time, her parents had talked of selling it and getting another place where there weren't so many outboards. This worried Rebecca, because she'd got to the age where hanging onto things that you loved made sense. But when the marriage failed, her parents sold it anyway, and neither of them bought anything new after that.

Right before the sale closed that February of her twenty-fifth year, Rebecca had gone up to spend a weekend alone in the cottage. If she ever felt low, she'd always found consolation in the little cabin with its panelled walls and its comforts. She lit a fire the first night and made herself toast for supper and sat near the grate, staring into the constantly warping shapes. Although the flame moved, the source of it was utterly still. The moment extended itself to encompass Rebecca as she was then, with the country home still in the family, and her young life still untouched by irreversible error. The night air was motionless outside the big window, and the lake frozen, and there was no one around for miles. It was a long deep shape of time, and it calmed her.

Diane came down the steps behind her, with a little cheddar sandwich on a white plate, a few grapes on the side. She handed the plate to Rebecca without a word, and then sat down in the chaise beside her. A big canvas umbrella blocked the late-day sun from their eyes.

Rebecca took small bites of the sandwich to be polite, then set it aside and lay back.

"Do you *vant* to be alone?" Diane said, and Rebecca laughed.

"No. I mean, I'm okay alone, if you want to be with the guys."

"You're a polite girl, Rebecca. It won't do."

"Stay, then."

The lake was flat in front of them, the islands across the way reflected in a green Rorschach on the surface. Silent ripples opened and closed on the lake surface, fish coming up to feed. Rebecca imagined tiny, serrated mouths blossoming all over, making holes in the surface, little pits with stomachs at the bottom. This was the kind of picture her mind offered up from time to time, an image that uncovered an ugly reality where someone else might only see something beautiful.

"There used to be a camp over on that side," said Diane, gesturing to a point on the other shore. "For underprivileged teenagers. They used to come in August for three weeks and canoe and have cookouts and shoot arrows."

"It's not open anymore?"

"They had a scandal. The last summer they were open, one of the girls let a friend who wasn't at the camp come in one night. The other girl drove in and parked in the trees back there. She had a newborn with her, maybe six days old, and she and her friend took out one of the canoes and paddled out to the middle—maybe 500 metres from here—and dropped the baby into the lake." She looked at Rebecca, who was smiling. "What?" she said.

"And now, every night, you can hear a baby crying somewhere out in the middle of the lake."

Diane ran her tongue over her teeth. "I thought it was true."

"It's not."

"It could be."

Robert called down. "Ten minutes!"

Diane waved.

"Are you and Robert okay?" said Rebecca. "Kevin told me things weren't going too well. I don't mean to pry."

Diane stretched her long legs out. They were brown from the sun, with a thin white crust of dry skin in some places, from an earlier tan. "Are we friends, Rebecca?"

"Oh," she said. "It's private. I'm sorry."

"Not if we're friends. If we're friends, you don't have to ask if you're prying."

"Okay."

"I had an affair." She let that hang for a moment. Rebecca didn't say anything, but she didn't look at Diane, either. "He didn't know until I told him, and I only told him because I wanted to give him a chance to leave if he wanted to. But then the bastard admitted he'd been having one, too. We were both cheating on each other." She looked over at Rebecca, and the fizzing started again in Rebecca's head, like a faint breathing behind her eyes—radio voices. "It's pretty easy to be rotten to the one you love," Diane said.

The waitress came and refilled Rebecca's cup. She was wearing slippers. It was still just her and the waitress in the restaurant, although Rebecca could see an old man sitting on a push-stool just inside the kitchen. He was smoking a cigarette.

"No, thank you," said Rebecca, waving away the offer of a creamer.

The old man in the kitchen exhaled a voluptuous chestful of smoke, and it went up in front of his face, obscuring it and imparting its colour to his skin.

"Is that your father?" Rebecca asked.

"He is the cook," said the waitress.

"He could be the cook *and* your father."

"My father does not cook here." She went away with the coffee. *Where does he cook, then?* Rebecca wanted to say, automatically slipping into the phraseology of the logic puzzles she'd loved as a kid: *The waitress' father does not cook at The Rickshaw. The man who doesn't smoke was not born in Guangzhou.* Her father had shown her how to fill in the grids, cancelling alternatives, accruing details that could not be true and leaving one possibility behind. When you sorted out a relationship, you put a checkmark at the intersection. *Two of the cooks are brothers, but the older brother is not the waitress' uncle.*

The waitress was in her forties or fifties; Rebecca couldn't tell. A wave of something came over her—it contained a whiff of despair. She knew the waitress went home alone, and so did the old man who was not her father. Rebecca imagined that this was the closest thing either of them had to a relationship. It was heartbreaking to consider the lots of people who had less hope than yourself, although, thought Rebecca, the recognition of others' pain was not enough to make her own seem manageable. In fact, sometimes it made her own suffering seem ridiculous, a feeling that brought a surfeit of pain.

The woman came back with the bill. Perhaps her personal question had triggered a decision that it was time to close. Rebecca looked up at the neon-lit clock and saw that it was already after midnight.

"I'll just finish this," she said.

"Take your time." The woman stayed close and cleaned the countertop lazily. She turned and wiped around the coffee machine, then took the carafe out from under the drip and poured the remaining coffee into the sink.

"I used to come here all the time, to Gravenhurst," she said to the woman's back. "My parents had a place on 169."

"We live in town," said the woman.

The *we* knocked Rebecca's imaginings askew, but she felt she couldn't ask the woman anything else about herself. She watched her continue to clean, her hand tracing light circles over the plasticized veneer, without enough pressure, it seemed, to pick anything off it but newspaper smudges. Maybe the *we* meant there was a mother or an elderly person to whom she was obligated, and the waitress was therefore not alone at all. Rebecca thought perhaps this woman would go back to wherever she lived and would be greeted by the smells of genuine cookery, the sort from the old country that they could not make in this café. The people who came here wanted omelettes or stir-fried bean sprouts with chicken and soy sauce—or coffee and lemon pie. When did people like herself and this woman ever reach across their boundaries to make a link? She could keep coming back here; even if Robert and Diane split up, she could keep coming back to this town where she'd spent the summers of her childhood, come into The Rickshaw and say hello to the waitress, whose name might be Lucy—such things as grew roots between two unlikely persons could be seeded here. She could meet Lucy's mother. She could take back to Toronto the clippings of alien houseplants and grow them in a window in her own kitchen.

The woman came back and looked down at the bill, and Rebecca said "oh yeah," and fumbled with her wallet. The waitress held up a hand.

"No hurry," she said.

When Rebecca and Diane went back up the steps to the cottage, Robert was slicing the beef into fragrant red slivers. Dark blood pooled underneath. Diane went and stood behind Robert and put her head on his shoulder so that it looked as if Robert had two heads. Rebecca felt the welling that had been building all evening finally begin to coalesce in the pit of her stomach, the warp of the unnameable taking its terrible shape, and her hands went cold. Kevin slipped an arm around her waist and kissed her neck and that was all the logic her mind needed and the little chambers of her heart fisted up and she was having an attack. She reeled off his arm and stood apart.

"Suck up, you're behind," said Robert. "Then we'll tuck into this." *Suck, tuck,* her mind went, wallowing in ominous connections. Robert ran the tip of a finger down the top edges of the meat, riffling it as though it was a deck of cards made out of flesh. *Life's Little Emergencies,* went her mind, and then, *Jack the Ripper.* Kevin was looking at her.

"You're still not right, are you?"

"I'm fine." She turned her attention to Robert. She was containing the shallow little breaths that lapped up against her ribcage. "So you guys are okay now? You and Diane?"

"*Comme la pluie,*" said Robert. "Except she's nuts."

Kevin laughed, and Robert leaned in toward Rebecca to tell her whatever it was Kevin already knew was funny. "We went out for a coffee the other night, she and me—"

Sheen me

"—and she farted out loud because there was only one other table there and they were all speaking German and she figured they wouldn't understand."

"HAW HAW," went Diane right into Robert's ear. She kissed his cheek and stepped toward the door. "I told Rebecca, by the way," she said. "You're not the only one with a nasty secret." She was holding the door open and Robert went in beside her with the blood-scented platter.

"A stalemate is also a way not to lose," he said over his

shoulder to Rebecca. "What do you think of getting married now?"

She'd gone in and sat down, but before she could be served she said she was still not feeling well. Maybe she was coming down with something; she wanted to rest some more. Kevin walked her back to the cabin, and she fell into the bed on her belly, the waves of panic still streaming through her, dark smoke without flame. He rubbed her back. "What's going on?"

"I think I'm feeling a bit overwhelmed." Her voice was little more than a whisper.

"You're hot. Why don't I get you a Tylenol?"

"You go," she said. "I'll be fine in a bit."

"We're not like them, you know."

She pushed herself up on her elbows. "What does that mean, Kevin? Why would you think I was worried about who I was like? Or who *we* were like?"

He pulled his face back, surprised. "I'm just picking up that they make you feel strange."

"*I* make me feel strange. But I'll deal with it. You go eat Sally Field or Bessie, or whatever Robert's named that fucking piece of meat." She flopped back down on the bed, and he put his hand on the small of her back again, and although this contact with him was just what she needed, she gently pushed the hand away. "Go on," she said.

He looked at her, a little hurt that she wouldn't reach out to him, but she never reached out to him; theirs was a relationship fuelled by a strenuous effort to be happy, and if not happy, then pleasant. In his mind, their relationship worked; this was why he wanted to buy a place with her, this was why (as he'd told Robert) he would shortly ask her to marry him. He leaned down and kissed her softly on the forehead, then went back into the cottage. She heard his footsteps receding and the spring-stretch of the door as he went in. Then she lay there, with the sound of roaring in her ears.

Taking tiny breaths, she got up, and dug into her toiletry kit and got out the bottle with the small blue pills in it. She hadn't needed one of these for more than a year. Having to take one felt like failure, as if all the time she spent between the need to reach for one was just a pause in the natural order, that order being one in which she couldn't cope, couldn't helm herself, was broken in a way not evident to anyone but her. She let one of the pills dissolve under her tongue into a wet sugary powder and within moments the sounds diminished and her skin began to lay down again along her arms and legs. She lay there breathing. Then the pill, with its mother's hands, stroked her to sleep.

She'd brought Kevin to meet her mother, earlier in the summer. They dropped in because they were "in the area," and they'd caught her baking for a party. So they pitched in, an impromptu comedy with Kevin trying to get edible silver balls to sit dead centre on the tops of a gross of sugar cookies, while Rebecca and her mother stuck toothpicks into pound cakes and whispered in the corner.

"Well?" she asked, and her mother replied that she wanted Rebecca to be happy. "That's the blessing of a pessimist."

"Is he a lot older than you?"

"*No*. He's a good guy, Mum. He's serious. He's had the same job for five years. He's principled."

"Is he funny? Your father was funny."

"*Is* funny," she said. She was watching Kevin trying to drop the candy decorations into their correct positions. "Look at him now." Her mother turned and smiled. The tip of his tongue was sticking out of the corner of his mouth. After a moment, he looked up at them and grinned.

"Two for them, one for me," he said, and put one in his mouth.

"Have you ever been married, Kevin?"

He looked from mother to daughter and back. "I've never been married," he said.

"Well, don't," said Rebecca's mother. "Our generation got it all wrong. We had sex and thought that if we got married the other person would start making sense. We thought marriage made you serious."

"You don't think it does," he said carefully. His parents were still married, and he'd talked about marriage with Rebecca in a circular fashion, theoretically, as if it were an intellectual hare rather than a possibility.

"Marriage makes you put your trust in an idea."

"It's a good idea for some people, though," he said. Rebecca leaned her hip against the countertop and pushed a fingertip through a dusting of flour there. "In any case, Ms. Jamieson, Rebecca and I are taking things slowly. Aren't we?"

Rebecca nodded and smiled, but didn't take her eye off her flour mandela. "Slow enough."

"But not so slow that you didn't teach him my maiden name."

"Well, you're not Mrs. Silver anymore, Mum."

Her mother covered her ears in mock horror. "Eee! My slave name!"

Kevin stood up and put the box of candy balls down on the counter. "It was great to meet you," he said.

When Rebecca woke it was dark out, and the covers had been folded back from the other side of the bed, over her body. She could hear the voices of her friends and her lover in the cottage, murmurs punctuated by laughter. She swivelled out of the bed and sat there, waiting for her senses to come online, then stood up and took the car keys off the dresser. She went out to the car and started the motor, and when, after two or three minutes, no one came out to stop her, she reversed down the long driveway and out onto the road.

The sky was blue-black and the stars hung in vast profusions, a pale river of them arcing through the emptiness. She drove into the town and through the town, and when she got to the highway that led back down toward the city, she turned north and drove to the little access road that went to the lake of her childhood. On the birches and pines that appeared in her headlights were the little handpainted signs of the families who had always been there, names of people she knew but had never met. Signs cut into animal shapes—turtles, frogs, bears.

In the ten years since, they'd paved the road that led to the shore where the old place was. Some new cottages had gone up in that time, crowding in along the treed edge of the lake, big satellite dishes drinking in the sky's signals. But her place was still there, and after she parked and got out, she could see it hadn't changed much at all. The current owners had kept the woodpile in the same place, and the flagstones that led down the middle of the property to the dock were the same ones she'd helped her father lay when she was a kid. She followed them down to the lake, where the moon lay like a ribbon across the water.

There was no other car parked beside the cottage, and there were very few lights on in the cottages nearby, so she imagined herself entirely alone with the place, that it was hers again. She stood on the dock and looked up at the brown shingled roof that sloped down over the broad windows, and she saw herself inside the cottage, looking out. There had been such a richness of days there—long days with their hours full—that it seemed a trick of time that her memories of it felt like they could be recounted in less than an hour.

The water lapped up on the underside of the dock. All

the life down there in the water, that she had taken such pleasure in as a child—the bright sunfish, the turtles anxious to escape a child's hand, batting away with tiny clawed feet. She took in all the smells (pine and lakewater and rained-on soil, sunned rocks, snake skin, the sweet scent of arbour); she slept in the cottage's beds and felt her way to the bathroom in the middle of the night, the palm of her hand brushing over the paper maps. She was seven, and ten, and fifteen, and then twenty-five here. She'd brought her first boyfriends here; her parents had trusted her with the keys. She'd shared ice creams and, later, bottles of wine on this very dock, this wood that had to know her better than anything that had come after. This was one place in the world where she belonged, even now, even though what it stood for, without any challenge from reality, had been long dispersed. This was the fate of all the things that stayed with you for too long. It was a form of good luck, this unnatural permanence, but it made the rest of life harder for you, getting used to the intemperate roil of ordinary change.

She got back into her car and pointed it in the direction she'd come, driving in the deep darkness by instinct. It was almost eleven when she got back to town.

The waitress took her coat from the hook under the counter and put it on. Rebecca had laid her money out, and when the woman picked it up said she didn't need change. It was a good tip; the woman could have left some time ago if not for Rebecca nursing her coffee.

She wondered if Kevin had gone into the cabin by now and found her missing. Or if the three of them had continued to open the bottles of wine that Robert kept under the cottage, and sat and talked, or looked at the photos they were all in. She realized that if Kevin knew she was missing, there would be some trouble when she got back. She'd have to explain this part of herself that she'd so far been able to keep apart from him. That he didn't know her the way he thought he did said something about her, but something about them as well. She'd kept this realization from herself.

"Joe still has to clean in the kitchen," said the waitress. She was holding a small white beaded purse in her hand. "You can stay until he goes, if you like."

"Is his name really Joe?"

"Everyone calls him that."

"But what's his real name?" she asked.

"It is Ming Kang. But I call him Joe as well."

"And your name?"

"Betty. Mei Li."

Rebecca watched her go into the kitchen and talk a moment with Joe, who looked out into the dining room and saw Rebecca for the first time. He nodded and lifted a hand in greeting to her, and she waved back, abashed. It was time for her to go, but part of her wanted to wait long enough to make a confrontation with Kevin necessary. She could not bring herself to tell her own truths by choice. She wanted to be forced.

Betty laughed at something Joe said, and then she

leaned down to him and kissed him on the lips, one hand resting on his shoulder. Joe watched her go and then turned his placid face back to Rebecca. In her mind, she drew a checkmark. *Mei Li, who is also called Betty, is the waitress and is married to Ming Kang, the cook, who is also called Joe.*

Now for the rest of it.

THE FLESH COLLECTORS

By forty-eight, Roth had had his midlife crisis, four children, and three wives, the last of whom was still interested in sex, but not in having babies, and who had developed a serious allergy to latex. It was bad enough that they were still using condoms at their ages (although, granted, Sybil was eight years younger than he and could still, theoretically, reproduce), but his wife had ruled out having any part of her body removed for the purposes of pleasure, since she believed, like most Jews, that it was crucial to go to the grave whole, or else when the Messiah came you might be walking around for eternity lacking a crucial component. A missing appendix was forgivable, and certainly anything that had to be shed for life-saving reasons was as well, just as it was not a sin to drink water on Yom Kippur if you had to take medication. "Doctor's orders," you'd hear someone saying in the synagogue hallway, pushing some capsule to the back of their throat and drinking long and deep from the fountain between the bathrooms.

The pill was absolutely out as well for Sybil, not because it was forbidden, but rather because it was apt to make her behave like a drugged monkey. Roth had often argued that some discomfort in the service of a happy marriage was an obligation to a good husband or wife, but

Sybil had turned this argument against him. This was why Roth was staring down the possibility that he would soon have to submit a tender part of himself to a surgeon's knife. Such an operation would leave him whole—it was more a sundering than a deletion—and so, in the sense intended by the ancients, his options were considerably less fraught than hers.

His GP, Arnold Gravesend, told him that vasectomies, in this day and age, were twenty-minute affairs and didn't even have to be done by scalpel. Still, the prospect of having this part of his body interfered with made Roth woozy. He'd been delaying for months now, and Sybil was withholding connubially and building a wifely case against him. "I don't feel like breaking out into a yeast infection every time, Nathan. We're not newlyweds anymore. If you care about our marriage, you'll do what you have to do."

In principle, Roth agreed. To his own thinking, condoms provided biblical loopholes for people who were otherwise happy to follow the laws. His rabbi, Stern of Beth Israel, said that condoms did not release their users from the burden of sin. It was still spilling semen in vain, said Rabbi Stern. The good Jewish couple knows when the woman is in season and takes advantage accordingly.

Roth had relaxed his own strictures as he'd got older. With Adele, his first wife, he didn't even sleep in the bed with her when she was in cycle (a holdover of custom from his orthodox upbringing, even though he considered himself conservative now), but after they'd divorced he decided to be more "humane," as the therapist had put it to him, back when there was a chance to save the marriage. There was no sense in treating the person you loved as an opportunity *not* to sin if it meant hurting their feelings for one week out of every four. This was excellent advice, and his second marriage, to a dark-eyed beauty named Lila he'd met at a bazaar, would have lasted for life if she hadn't died. "The Cancer," Lila's mother had called it, as if there had been only one cancer in the whole world and it struck her daughter. At the funeral, she'd keened over and over again, *Why did we name her for the night?* "Lila" was Hebrew for night, a time when Roth's soul was always calm.

Sybil was a North Toronto woman. Not exotic, and street- rather than book-smart, but for Roth, it was time to slow down anyway and to lead a simpler life. Everything but his sexual urges, which frequently troubled him, had come to a better balance. He'd blown his relationships with his first two children, from Adele, but the last two, with Lila, were still growing up and hadn't yet learned to view him as an old fool. (That he wasn't old, not really, was of no consequence to the first two, to whom he suspected he'd been old since he was thirty.) As time went on, Roth seemed to fill with more love for his own children than he'd ever thought he could feel, and there was still a chance to hold Lila's and his children in the goodness of this love. These two still lived with him, ten-year-old Mitchell and his younger sister Sarah. Roth was all they had of their mother. They treated Sybil like an intruder and took his side in everything.

"Are you going to your doctor?" Sybil had asked at breakfast.

"Are you sick, Daddy?"

He was going to reply to his son, but Sybil turned her moisturized face toward the child and said, "There is nothing wrong with your father that can't be fixed in ten minutes."

"Is this the snip-snip?"

His sister, her spoon dripping with milk coloured by her cereal, looked up with her eyes creased. "What's the snip-snip?" she asked.

"I'm perfectly healthy, you guys," Roth said. "There's nothing wrong with me. And we don't use words like 'snip-snip' at the kitchen table."

"I can't remember the real word," said the boy.

Sybil collected her and Roth's plates and lay them in the sink. She didn't do dishes. The girl did the dishes. Roth hated having a maid, especially one that didn't live with them. It seemed to strip the position of any residual dignity it may have had, by forcing her to show up every morning to sweep through the house, and return every evening to whatever cramped squalor she no doubt lived in. "Vasectomy," said Sybil. The word caused a metallic wave of energy to run down Roth's spine, as if every bone in his body had been rubbed with aluminum foil.

"What is *that*?" said Sarah with disgust.

"It means Daddy won't be able to make a baby anymore," he said.

"Why?"

Sybil ruffled the little girl's thin black hair. "Because step-mummy doesn't want any kids."

"Oh," said his daughter. He'd already told her and Mitchell how reproduction worked. Rabbi Stern said it was all right to be explicit with children, as long as they were aware that the mysteries of sex were more important than its mechanics. Always foreground the wonders of the great fabric of life, said Stern. Roth had sought his advice less and less in recent years. *I've had divorce and death*, he thought. *It sounds like God's already made up his vast mind about me.*

When he'd sat down to talk with the children, he did so without the aid of a book or pen and paper. He simply told them the raw facts. What happened in the man's body, in the woman's. How it actually worked, sex. And after. The baby, inside, growing. They were fascinated. This was when Lila was still alive. It was the four of them, inviolate. The children got used to the fact that their parents had touched in that way. It made them all magical.

Now they considered that their father did much the same thing with their stepmother. Mitchell had some sense that it was not just for making children, and the snip-snip confirmed this. Their father wanted to stop having children for good, but he still wanted to put his penis inside their stepmother's vagina. Something else must be going on, thought the boy, like a hidden level in a video game.

Roth and Sybil got the children ready for the bus and saw them off up at the corner. She linked her arm in his. "I'm sorry," she said.

"What for."

"This whole operation thing makes you uncomfortable, and I'm being pushy. Forgive me. If you do it, you'll do it when you're ready, and from now on, I'll be *schtum*."

"*Schtum* and you have never been that close, Sybil. But thank you. I am going to do it, though. I will."

"I know you will," she said, and she squeezed his arm tight to her body. "Then you can have me at the drop of a hat, Mr. Roth."

He had to admit, there was an imperishable upside to the whole thing, and that was the thought of the entire garden of Sybil's body, open at all hours. He'd always been able to admit to himself that where his relationships were concerned, lust had always been a factor. Even the dourest rabbis of history would have told you no man or woman marries for the mere sake of a likeness of mind or spirit. How else to make you "as numerous as the stars in the heavens"? Such a covenant could not be accomplished without giving men and women the benefit of appetites. Roth had never had it in short supply. For a man whose external life had been as dull as the need for money can make it (he operated a company called Storage Solutions), his true life, his inner life, was lush. With Adele it had perhaps been wasted a little: the impatience and artlessness of youth. But with Lila. They'd worn the hinges off each other. Unlike many of the women he'd known then, she didn't care for the strictest of the laws, and she wore jeans and T-shirts. She dressed for comfort. Seeing her walking around the house in the uniform of the pagan world inflamed Roth terribly. He thought it was pathetic that something as banal as blue-jeans could do this to him, but desire blossoms in forbidden soil. He imagined that the sight of the tip of a woman's nose would have a similar effect on his Moslem brethren. As long as husband and wife could be kind to each other, the prohibited was the seedbed of passion.

Roth's uncertainty about his options (he would never have used the word *bewilderment*) brought him to Beth Israel, to see Rabbi Stern. Roth had long since given up on making sense of the many laws that were to govern his life and his behaviour. These things had been drummed into him as a child, which was part of the reason he had strayed, although straying from orthodoxy to conservativism was a deviation on the order of dark rye to light. In any case, much of what he once thought he knew was now so much clutter in his mind. Stern had admonished him about his confusion many times: Roth was dangerously close to leading an unguided—and therefore impious—life.

Stern's study at the temple was cluttered and dark. Only a fish tank that took up one whole wall provided a useful light. Going into the Rabbi's office was like descending into an underground exhibit, with its blue glow and its undulating creatures moving back and forth behind glass.

"Sybil wants me to have a vasectomy," said Roth once he'd sat down.

"You have a problem with this?"

"No, not really." The rabbi unwrapped a candy and left the silvery paper on the tabletop. He waited for Roth. "My problem is that I've had three wives. How do I know this is the last one? What if I need—?"

"What if you need your *sperm*?"

"Yes."

"Mmm," said Stern. "You love Sybil?"

"Yes."

"So? Have a vasectomy. You're almost fifty, Nathan; Sybil's almost forty. It's over for children."

Roth nodded. It wasn't really about loving Sybil, though. It was about the future, and what it might want from him. What if, one day, it wanted him to start over, not as a husband, but as a father? What if he blew it this time too, with Mitchell and Sarah? "What if I *want* more children, though?" he said.

The rabbi leaned forward. He regarded Roth as one would look into a cloudy puddle, to judge its depth. "What are you thinking, Nathan?"

"I want to save some of my sperm. In case."

"You can't do that."

"Why."

Stern lifted his large hands off the table and let them

drop back down. The noise startled Roth; they made a sound like two mallets falling. "Either you commit the sin of Onan, or you commit adultery—and not just a garden variety adultery my friend—one you're *planning*. This is like the same difference between first- and second-degree murder."

"I thought it was a *mitzvah* to have children, Rabbi. To repopulate the land."

Stern extended a hand toward Roth as if it held an offering. "Here, Nathan. You go to some place that will freeze your sperm, and if that sperm is not used to make a baby, then you've spilled it in vain. *But*—" and here he held out the other hand "—let's say you *intend* to make a baby with that sperm. We already know it's not going anywhere near Sybil. Correct?"

"Yes."

"*So,* this sperm is intended for *another* woman. That's your premeditated sin, Roth. This is not good."

Roth stood up then, irritated enough to raise his voice. "Look—"

"—sit down," said the rabbi.

"Can't you just advise me as a man? Either I do this thing that makes me a bad person, or I go crazy. You tell me."

"Don't do it, Nathan," said Stern. "It's not for me to tell you to go flush your soul down the toilet so you can have your cake and eat it too." He stared at Roth a moment, blinking. "You know what I mean."

Sweat slicked Roth's back. What had he thought the

man was going to tell him, anyway? He shook the rabbi's
hand.

"You've made up your mind?"

"I don't know," said Roth.

Is there much difference, Roth wondered, between a
person who is interested in your money and one who is
interested in your soul? Should you automatically assume
that the second person is looking out for you? From his
years of working in a retail environment, Roth was sure
he knew a great many more fulfilled people among those
who had placed their faith in business, rather than in God.
Money had a reassuring finiteness to it; money didn't get
ambiguous or allegorical on you. And although he
understood, abstractly, that money *was* a metaphor, it was
still true that if something cost ten dollars and you had ten
dollars, you could have it. It didn't seem to work that way
in the Kingdom of Heaven. The news from up there was
that through hard work and application you could ruin
your first marriage, but then you could have a second
chance, and you could even have two more lovely
children and do it right this time. But then you could lose
it all over again. If you invested your soul at ten per cent
compounded over fifty years, you could still have nothing
in the end.

Roth knew that this kind of talk was just some bitter
kind of Hebraic stand-up routine that looped through the
mind of anyone who'd lost something or someone
important to them. It went all the way back to the Tribes

of Israel in the desert outside of Egypt, when God said, *Guess what? You're not slaves no more. Congratulations. Oh, by the way, did I mention the desert? Forty years only, without nothing to eat except crackers and scorpions? I thought maybe I didn't say the desert part.* No doubt that when they finally got there—the Land of Milk and Honey—half got diarrhea from the milk, and the other half went into anaphylactic shock from the honey. No, blind faith was a bad thing, and perhaps the elders were just elders, a little confused from centuries of trying to figure out the worth of an oxen. Roth was smart to go it alone.

As it was, he'd already had the advice of the vasectomist. He'd made and actually kept an appointment some weeks earlier. He'd gone to the doctor's office, out in the east end, and kept his eyes down in the waiting room filled with other men. There was a receptionist whose hair was the only thing that showed over the countertop. The sound of unread pages being turned was the only noise in the place, except for the occasional invitation to someone to go see the doctor. Then they'd come out and huddle over the desk with the secretary, and most of them, at one point, would offer a nervous laugh, then take their coat and leave.

When it was his turn, Roth went in and sat in the doctor's private office. It had all the soothing ornaments a doctor's office is supposed to have: the signed documents, the wood panelling, the framed pictures with their backs turned like embarassed party guests. The only thing out of place was the big plastic testicle on the doctor's desk. This he used to demonstrate the brief, painless procedure with the brief, only slightly uncomfortable recovery period. Roth tried to pay attention to the big nut with its removable layers and tubes, but all he could hear the doctor say, at least three times, was, "Then we make a very small incision here."

"I thought there was a method that didn't require an incision," said Roth.

"Well, some doctors use a puncture method that's more like making a little hole through which the vas deferens is extracted, but it's essentially the same thing, Mr. Roth. You have to get into the scrotum somehow, and from there it's a cruel cut no matter how you look at it." He'd taken the top layer off to show the blue vas deferens beneath, and now he pulled the vas apart in the middle. It split into two with a neat little *click*.

Roth nodded. "I see."

"Do you have any more questions?"

"Can it be reversed?"

The doctor sighed dramatically and looked away from Roth, tapping the denuded testicle with the tip of his pen. Roth saw now that the top of the plastic model was stippled with pen marks. "If you are concerned with reversal, Mr. Roth, you may want to think harder about your reasons for seeking vasectomy. Are you sure they're *your* reasons? The point of a vasectomy is to take the bullets out of the chambers, so to speak. If you think you're going to want to use live ammo again, then maybe this isn't for you."

"I just want to know what my options are."

"Some doctors undo it," he said curtly. "I don't. It's not *meant* to be undone." He brusquely reassembled the model, snapping the two ends of the vas deferens back together and covering it with the scrotal sac. "And it's not this easy, either," he said.

Back out at the reception, the woman gave him a nice smile and stood up.

"Will you be making an appointment, Mr. Roth?"

"Yes," he said quietly. She looked down behind her desk and removed two sheets of paper, which she spun toward him so that he could read them. She pointed out what he needed to know with the tip of a pencil.

"No anti-inflammatories for ten days before the procedure," she said, "so no Aspirin or Advil, you know. Tylenol is okay." He nodded dumbly. "Make sure there's someone here to pick you up afterwards, and remember to bring this form—" here she brought out the second sheet "—which is a consent form you have to sign saying you understand the risks and that we don't guarantee sterility."

"It's not guaranteed?"

"Well, it is," she said, "but by law we have to put that. And will you be paying for prep or would you like to prep yourself?"

"I'm sorry?" Roth said.

"Someone here can shave the area for you, at a nominal cost, or you can do it yourself."

His mouth was dry. "I'll do it myself."

"Very good," said the receptionist, folding his information and slipping it into an envelope. "Just make sure you don't do the whole operation by accident."

Roth laughed nervously.

It seemed to him that in all the years he'd been seeing doctors the luxury of a bedside manner was one rarely found. If you weren't really that sick, it was a quick scribble on a piece of paper and out you went, there were sicker people than you. But if you *were* truly ill, if there was no hope for you, it was worse. Dead customers are no good for any business. When Lila had taken ill, he'd been amazed at the clinical distance they encountered at their various stops on the road to her death. It had got so bad that Roth wanted to strangle some of them. *What would it cost for a little comfort?* But Lila kept herself in check. She wanted to save her strength.

Little bits of her went off regularly to be tested. Cell counts and biopsies. The children didn't understand why their mother was losing weight. She told them she was tired from the sickness and didn't need as much to eat as she did before, but Roth knew it was because they were taking her away, biopsy by biopsy. Stern had been cold comfort here as well.

"She'll go to her death half the woman she once was," he'd complained to the rabbi. "And you tell me it's still kosher with the *meshiach*?"

"God's not going to keep Lila out of the Promised Land

because she had a few operations. It doesn't work that way."

"Then how *does* it work?"

Stern stood up then, his face dark with worry. "Nathan, you need to go and be with her and with your children and stop worrying about the next life. She needs you."

He was shaking. "Do I keep everything they take out of her, Rabbi? Does it all get buried with her?"

"The cancer isn't *her*. And it's not the point, Nathan. It's a metaphor, this whole thing. You want to present yourself to God as an *entire* human being, not just a complete body. Think about it like that."

This was what was in Roth's mind as he drove north through midtown to the clinic he'd found in the Yellow Pages. The clinic was beyond where he'd grown up, clear beyond all the Reform synagogues with their big lawns and *goyish*-looking stained-glass windows. It was in a strip of offices beside a tennis club, a non-descript building with a sign on the door that said simply, FDS Technologies.

There was no one in this waiting room, and the secretary sat at a desk, where it was easy to make eye contact.

"Mr. Roth," she said. He was right on time. She stood up and came around the desk to shake his hand. "Why don't I take your jacket and you can fill out a few forms. Then we'll go in."

He took the forms from her and sat. He couldn't

imagine how he was going to provide a sample; there was nothing about the place that made it likely. The lady took the clipboard back from him after she saw him sign it.

"It's two hundred dollars the first year and seventy-five for every year afterwards. That's for one vial. It's half-price for every vial after that."

"How many vials do most people give?"

"Oh, that's a personal decision, Mr. Roth. Some people give two or three, and some even come back after that and give a few more. It's whatever you think you'll need, and whatever you're comfortable with."

The image of the back rooms behind her desk filled with men on return visits filled Roth with disgust. Did some people treat this as a hobby? This last-ditch, strip-mall, storage facility? At least the place he ran had pretty signage and he could look his customers in the eye. "I think I'll just be doing the one."

"All right then."

"It's in case of . . ." He hunted in his wallet for a credit card. "I probably won't ever need it."

"If you ever get to the point where you want us to dispose of the vial, we do that at no extra charge."

"Can somebody else use it?"

"I'm not sure what you mean, Mr. Roth."

"Maybe for medical research. Or for a couple who can't have one on their own."

"We can't pass along unwanted specimens, I'm sorry. You can have it back if you choose, but otherwise we destroy it."

This information sent Roth into a strange revery, this notion that he could have his own sperm back. He imagined himself, perhaps twenty years down the road, a vasectomized man about sixteen hundred dollars out-of-pocket, finally returning to FDS Technologies to reclaim his specimen, and then onward to one of the doctors in town who actually did reversals, where he'd have his tubes reconnected and his own sperm put back into his own testicles. How he'd laugh at the rabbi then. *Who's a sinner now, Stern?*

"Mr. Roth," the receptionist repeated. "If you'll come with me?"

He followed the woman down a hall of doorways. To the clinic's credit, they had not decorated the walls with pictures. What do you put on a wall in such a place? Everything could be taken the wrong way.

The woman was approaching a door with a blue plastic tag on it. She turned it around on its hook to its red side and opened the door with a key. "For your privacy, Mr. Roth, the lock on the other side of this door, once you turn it, locks the room from the inside. So you can relax knowing there is no way that anyone can enter."

She pushed the door open and they went inside. There was a single bed and a La-Z-Boy chair, in a space that looked like a very nice bachelor apartment. There was a bookshelf with a few books on it (no erotic masterpieces, noted Roth, seeing the names Deighton and King), and there were a couple of cabinets and a television hanging from a steel pole in the ceiling. The receptionist put a glass vial down on a desk beside the door.

"Now, this room is yours, Mr. Roth, for as long as you like. In that cabinet over there—" she pointed to the space below the television "—are some items you may feel you need, and many men do use them, so please feel free. Don't be embarrassed. This is the business we're in and the thing we really want is a good, healthy specimen to be put aside and kept for future use, so it's important to relax and let your body do what it knows how to do. That's the way you get your money's worth. Now, some men prefer to take a nap and take advantage of one of those wonderful things about their physiology, and just do what they need to do as soon as they wake up. This is why we ask you to come in when you've got at least five free hours—that way you can nap if you like."

Roth listened carefully, nodding as if someone were telling him how to operate a new and interesting machine. He felt curiously empty, as though he'd somehow signed away all his worldly possessions and he was the only thing that remained of his life. The receptionist was explaining that there were normal television channels and normal books, everything you might need to feel that you're on a little vacation. She held out her hand and Roth took it with a fixed smile.

"Most men laugh when I say good luck, but good luck." Roth broadened his smile. "To get to the last thing, the actual placement of the specimen, we really do recommend that you use one of the sterilized condoms that you'll find in the drawer beside the bed and only worry about getting the specimen into the bottle once you've got it. So don't get all knotted up over the mechanics of aiming or anything like that. All right, then?"

Roth was still holding the woman's hand. "All right," he said, and she went out and he turned the big silver lock to the left and stood alone in the quaint, anonymous room.

A half-hour later, Roth lay under the covers in the little bed, thinking maybe he'd drowse. He'd told Rachel, his manager, that he was not going to be available all afternoon owing to the fact that he was having minor day surgery, something to do with his dermatologist and some liquid nitrogen. Sybil never called him at work, so there was little worry that he'd later have to square anything with her. At the very least, he wouldn't have to square the details, since Rachel hadn't asked for any, dermatological procedures being the kind of thing people were not so naturally curious about.

He had spent the better part of twenty minutes utterly failing to accomplish something he'd been doing successfully since before his bar mitzvah. The banal fantasies he'd called to action lacked any erotic dimension, and he'd lain in the bed feeling squalidly lonesome. His imaginings had segued within five minutes to a fantasy in which he was in front of a Russian firing squad, his pants around his ankles, and he would be shot if he did not bring himself to orgasm. This was an involving fantasy, but it had no power to bring about the required reaction, so he'd stopped altogether. So far his experience at FDS Technologies (*A Public Company*, he'd noted on the form he had to fill out) had veered between horror and despair.

Beside the bed was an array of switches, and he experimented with them until one dropped the room into darkness. Being less aware of where he was might help, he thought, and he settled himself down into the bed again. In the jet darkness, he couldn't see anything at all, but he was suddenly more aware of the workings of the building: the air being shuttled from one space to the next, overhead lights somewhere near, coolly buzzing, and even conversation, distant and with a hollow bass-line, maybe even in the restaurant three doors down from where he was. Nevertheless, he closed his eyes and focused, and began to build himself an imaginary woman. She was wearing a one-piece red bathing suit and her legs were oiled with lotion. The straps coming off her shoulders barely contained her breasts. She was darkly tanned, and her hair was raven black. Roth had her slip the bathing suit off, one shoulder at a time, peeling it over her chest and down her belly. She gracefully brought out one foot and then the other, gestures that he found stirring. Then she stood there naked in front of him, her legs open a little, one fist on a cocked hip, a sun-kissed Amazon.

She was beginning to work for him; Roth kept his eyes squeezed shut and moved a hand into place. But the moment he made contact with himself, the Amazon's breasts began to sag and the nut-brown nipples enlarged and became uneven. Her hair went sandy blonde, and dark lines appeared below her navel, rivulets of flesh that swam down toward her pubic hair. The long, thin legs thickened, and puckered flesh popped out on her thighs. Roth tracked his gaze up her body—the loved, imperfect body—and reached Lila's sad face. She was smiling at him, the smile meant to reassure him. She put her hands on his chest, spreading her fingers so that his hair sprouted between them, a forest of grey in the interstices of her long brown fingers. And she put her mouth to him, taking him in, enclosing and containing him, and he died there. She could not contain him, he could not allow that, although he had wished the best of him, the most vital parts of himself, could have done that for her.

He opened his eyes on the darkness again and fumbled for the light. The room blinked into existence around him, the sterile replica of a warm and homey space. What kind of sin was it that not only was he about to spill his seed in vain (with his luck), but that he appeared to want to commit the infidelity that Rabbi Stern had spoken of with his dead wife?

He pushed the covers back with his feet, shoving them off the bed. He was not tired enough to nap and had no faith, anyway, that he'd wake up in a state of physiological readiness, as the receptionist had so admiringly suggested.

Roth went into the bathroom and splashed some water on his face. He was surprised to see how red his cheeks were. Then he went back out and, without a pause in his step, he strode over to the cabinet under the hanging television. The items the receptionist had referred to were here, magazines printed on a paper stock much glossier than in any of the magazines he read. He dared not touch them, sharply aware of the duties they'd been pressed into by other clients of FDS Technologies. Despite their glossiness, he was not sure how easily such things wiped clean. On top of the magazines was the television converter; a thin strip of paper taped to the bottom of it said, simply, "Channel 55." Roth switched on the television and found it was tuned to Channel 11. Haltingly, he went up the dial, station by station, pausing on all the soap operas and the home shopping and the midday movies. He passed all the cable stations he and Sybil watched in the evenings and was surprised to see that their midday programming was just as interesting. They showed yet more of the dangerous car chases and explorations of distant ecologies that were their nighttime specialties.

When he got to 54 (a channel that specialized in foreign sports), Roth paused, his eyes feeling heavy and his breathing tight, then he switched to 55. There, a bright pink surface moved rhythmically to a musical score that might have been written for a bad spy film. He knew he was looking at a body, or bodies, and after a moment he made out that the largest object on the screen was the back of a woman's leg, which she herself was holding up (he could make out her forearm at the top of the screen, tucked under the back of her knee), and therefore, following down, the expected anatomies came into view.

The camera changed angle, and now it was clear what Roth was looking at. Neither performer wore anything, although the woman still had on a pair of socks. He stared at the image, under which he could make out the repetitive sounds of the man's effort and the woman's apparent pleasure, and felt his body respond. Now he could probably do it, as long as he was quick about it and didn't think too much and didn't take his eyes off the television. This was why the La-Z-Boy was positioned the way it was, about six feet from the cabinet, since you could tilt it back and be right in the eyeline of the television. But whereas Roth could count on the bed-sheets having been changed, the chair was upholstered, and nothing could compel him to sit down on it. Instead, he gingerly lowered his pants, put the converter on the floor, took a deep breath, and the man on the television withdrew himself from his partner and spilled himself in vain all over her face.

"For Christ's sake!" shouted Roth, completing some kind of sin circuit, and he reached down violently for the remote as the woman on the screen began massaging the vainly spilled fluids into her chest and neck. "Lord, Lord," Roth groaned, pushing the buttons to switch the images off. He pressed the power button, but nothing happened. He whacked the device against his leg in fury, stumbling backwards and wrenching his pants up. But this somehow turned up the volume so that the murmured sounds of approval coming from the woman filled the room with a low, wet growling. Roth's arms and legs went cold and he was afraid he might black out. He went right up under the television and jumped up to hit the power switch on the console, and on his second try, the converter slipped from his hand and hit the floor and the batteries spilled out. At the same moment, the channel changed as well, and Roth was looking at a news report from the Middle East.

He let his shoulders drop and he exhaled, his heart still squeezing madly inside his chest. He would not do this; he knew it now. This last moment in his life when his body might have had some role in the future had passed. He got down on the floor and started to look for the batteries, then had to sit up on his haunches to collect his air again. The sound from the television was encompassing; he was sure they could hear it three doors down. Instead of a hyperventilating woman, it was now an American newscaster's voice filling the room.

Someone had blown up a bus in Haifa. Above Roth's head, yellow tape flapped in close-up at the perimeter of the scene. The newscaster's voice numbered the casualties and reported that the work of the police had just begun. The camera closed in on the cramped space of the disaster, the shattered form of the bus at its centre, bits of red steel pointing up nakedly. The police stood outside the tape while men in green and white uniforms wandered the site, their hands protected by surgical gloves. The voice swarmed the air around Roth with its urgency, identifying the men as orthodox Jews appointed as representatives of the community, there to gather anything that looked like human remains for the sake of religious burial. They were allowed access to such disasters to do holy duty, combing with their bodies bent double the dark little spaces where someone's hand might have come to rest, where a strip of flesh might be clinging to a shard of glass like a flag. All of this went into their bags, to be blessed and returned to the earth where, at some longed-for moment in the future, the Angel of Mercy would open the graves and gather the assembly of the chosen, recreating their shattered bodies from remains.

Roth watched the scene numbly, his hands limp at his sides, his ears pulsing with the sounds of the ruined street. And as the men continued their terrible work, moving slowly back and forth over the smoking street, he realized they were calling his name, they were saying, *Roth, Roth*, over and over. They believed he was there. He was the only survivor and they were calling for him. *Roth!* they were calling. Hearing his name spoken like that made a strange kind of sense to him, and it filled his head with brightness, it made him feel like he was carrying a charge.

"I'm here," he said quietly, standing and stepping back so they could see him. He raised his arms; the men were frantically searching for him now, shouting *Roth, can you hear us?* His face lit up with hope, it glistened, he could hear them, they must be close now. He called out to them: "Here I am! I'm here!"

But despite answering them, they continued to look. What if they did not find him? What if he perished here, despite their efforts, what if he died under this great weight and he never again saw the children who still loved him? He would never fix then what was wrong in his life; his love would never grow to gather in his other children, the ones he'd lost, or grow to tie Sybil to him more perfectly. He would never have the chance to accept that he would grow older now, his strength would wane; here he would die at an age people would say was too young, and he didn't want that—he *was* too young, he still had much of his old vitality, he could have been a father again at this age if he'd wanted! All of this would fade from him, and he from it if the men gave up, and he cried out in desperation now, "HERE I AM!" until finally the door behind him was forced open and a security guard stood in the verge with the woman from the reception and they called out to him over the din. But Roth could not hear them; his attention was fastened to the flesh collectors. He was waiting until one of them turned and finally saw him there and reached out a gloved hand to deliver him to safety.

HUMAN ELEMENTS

As sometimes happens, I had a depression. It ought to be reassuring to know that half of humankind has had one, and there they all are, up and walking around again. It ought to be.

The best way to describe depression is that it can take seven hours to do a load of laundry. If you drink while you're doing the laundry, it will take eight, but it will seem to go faster, and you won't mind so much the red stains on your whites, or at least it will not seem to you to be confirmation of the hopelessness of everything.

Before I was depressed, I had mostly been lonesome. I was lonesome with people and without them. This condition led to my moving out of a house I'd been sharing with a woman named J—. I took a bachelor apartment in a university neighbourhood, and my loneliness metastasized. As winter came on, I realized that I was planning on dying there. I started to smoke, a disgusting habit, and I drank more. On the weekends, I went to loud parties thrown by the fraternities on my street. It was easy enough to walk into one and claim I was from another frat or another school, and someone would point out the keg and that was that. I brought home what my mother would once have called co-eds, and did the kinds of things that one was supposed to do with co-eds. It was a pleasant routine, but I'd already become immune to beauty, and once that happens, you're almost there. I'd been cured of the mating sickness that had always animated my life and I imagined my death would be like a plant drying out on a radiator, seemingly gradual, but ending with an ashy spasm. In all, it was an excellent plan, but then the spring came and the park beside the building filled up with children in strollers and the sun rose earlier and set later, and worse, spring training started and on every channel ballplayers were talking in the idiom of stupid but irrefutable hope. The black flame flared down and I came back to the dessicated kernel of my self. And, like a sign of life, simple loneliness came back. I decided to get out of the city.

In those days, I was still a poet. When I was with J—I wrote a great deal of poetry, but I never published it. I poured it into one black hard-covered notebook after another. J— thought I was keeping a diary and it freaked her out. She'd never met a man who kept a diary. I told her it was poetry, and no, she couldn't see it. So she came to believe I was writing things about her anyway, and in a sense I was. So I stopped, and poetry left me like a chronic condition suddenly clearing up. Although in the case of poetry, I would have been happy to go on suffering.

I left my little apartment in the university district and rented a cabin on a lake outside of tourist country, three hours north of the city. My thought was that I could start writing poetry again, and if that didn't work, at least I could smoke and read. There was no phone. Trying to live without a phone can make you realize how weird it is to be "modern." In a place where a phone never rings it starts to feel like someone's dropped you into a hole, although all it means is that you're in nature.

I found, for a few days, that talking to myself was reassuring. A human voice is a human voice. I didn't indulge in real dialogue; I wasn't crazy anymore, so there was no *Well, Russell, how are we this morning?* Or *Ha ha, good one Russell.* I just narrated my day to myself. *It's a beautiful morning,* I'd say. *Time for coffee.* I'd talk to my books. *Mr. Sorel,* I said to Stendhal's misanthropist, *make up your fucking mind.* And at night, down at the lakeshore, in the web of animal calls and the unseen water lapping against the rocks, I'd look up and name the alarming sky. Orion, Cassiopeia, Gemini. Constellations of the north. Even most of the sky was hidden from my sight.

I tried to write poems, but mainly I sat on the porch looking down the unkempt lawn to the ridge. Below the ridge, the land fell away in scrub and blackberry canes to the water. Pine trees and oaks were scattered all over the property, and a variety of birds visited the branches and performed their various tasks. I'd spent my summer childhood in places like this, under curving skies and jumping into lakes with the shadows of black branches laid on their surfaces. Outside of the city, my natural existential skittishness faded somewhat, even though the country can make you feel awesomely tiny, with its skies and wilderness. It was true I felt alone, I did crave another human voice. But at least I was supposed to feel alone there. After another couple of weeks passed, I stopped speaking to myself and slipped into a peaceable silence.

One morning around this time, I went outside to the porch with a cup of coffee, a plate of fried eggs, and the poems of Francis Ponge. When I looked up after an hour or so, I saw that there was something sticking up beyond the ridge. It looked as if someone had leaned a large piece of wet cardboard against it. I put down my book and walked to the edge of the porch, and in the changing perspective I saw I was looking at the top of a tent.

I stood there for a while, reassured to be in a space that was clearly defined as my own, but then I told myself I had nothing to fear and I went inside to grab a couple of friendly-gesture beers and walked down to the ridge. A pot of coffee sat on a portable gas stove to one side of the tent, and a duffel bag poked out of the front flap. On the other side was a large plastic tub with a lid on it; the faint sound of water moving around came from inside it. I continued down onto the thin line of grey sand that passed for the beach there, and off to the left, standing on the shore and peering down into the weeds, were a man and a woman. They each wore a headset with a microphone that arced over their mouths. They looked like a pair of badly lost telemarketers. I held up the beers and they exchanged glances, then the man looked at his watch and shrugged and they both came over.

"Thanks," said the woman. She was dressed in a well-rounded yellow bikini, and he was wearing a Speedo and a worn-out T-shirt that said *Be Kind to Your Mother* and had a big picture of the planet on it. He was over six feet, and terminated in a patch of thorny black hair. He was also comprehensively pierced. Neither of them made any move to explain what they were doing on my rented property. Finally, I said, "What are you doing here?"

"Oh, I'm Kate," said the woman, "and this is Sylvain. We're on a ministry capture." I stared at her blankly, so she added, "Frogs. We're catching and counting frogs for the Ministry of the Environment."

"I see," I said. "Well, nice to meet you. I'm Russell."

"Thanks for the beers, Russell. Are you a cottager?"

Given that she was in a bikini catching frogs for the government, I felt free to say, "I'm writing poetry in a rented cabin to get over a breakup."

Sylvain lifted his head a little. "Is it working?"

"I don't think so."

"Too bad," he said.

"But you're not in *that* place, are you?" Kate gestured with the beer bottle to the roof of the cabin. It was all we could see.

"I am. Why."

"See?" she said angrily to Sylvain. She really was quite lovely. Her long brown hair swayed up and covered her face for a moment when she swung her head over to him. She was a good foot shorter than he was. "So you're wondering what we're doing here?"

"It's okay," I said. "It's not really my place."

"We were told there wasn't anyone here. Otherwise, we would have introduced ourselves."

"As a courtesy," said Sylvain.

"I won't report you," I said. That seemed to make us equals again, and Sylvain raised his bottle to me before draining it. Kate put her bottle down in the cool muck at the shore.

"I'll bring them both up later, okay?" she said. Sylvain was already walking back along the bushes, his head down, his eyes sweeping back and forth like a metal detector. Kate whispered, "We just took a break."

"Well then, back to the mines."

She waved to me with her fingers, then went to join Sylvain. One of them had smelled like coconut and I was pretty sure it was her.

In my time in the north, I'd been trying to force diligence on myself in a vain effort to get some creative results. I'd been starting my days with whiskey-splashed coffee and reversing the ratio as the day went on, and this might have been playing a role in my output. It certainly had a deleterious effect on my ability to read. I'd come armed with enough books to last me my stay, but, especially after lunchtime, I had trouble understanding what exactly was happening on the page. I would see the words, and I'd *hear* them in my head, and for the first time in my life, that seemed like a very odd thing. If I saw the word H-U-M-A-N-I-T-Y, I would hear *hyoo-MAN-itty*, and I realized those two things were not the same. There was some filter that caused what was out in the world to make a sound in my head. And so I became frightened of reading and had no other agenda after that except to write, and that was not going well, either. It was a relief, then, that some hint of human activity was taking place down by the water. It relaxed me.

The morning after the frog-catchers' appearance, I once again took my coffee and my notebook out to the porch. They had already left for their work, creeping through the reeds at the lake perimeter, armed with a couple of clipboards. I put out a cigarette and opened the notebook. I'd written two lines of what I presumed was poetry since I'd got there, about three weeks earlier. There were also some drawings of tree limbs and my own hand. The two lines of poetry were:

quadrabalance of the elements
human limbs, months, and hours

I wasn't sure what they were leading to, what they meant, or even if they were mathematically accurate. At least they didn't sound like conversation, so I wasn't going to give up quite yet. I'd always felt that if I didn't know exactly what I was doing, there was still a chance I'd write something worth the time it took to write anything.

Below, I heard someone splashing along the water's edge and then, I presumed, come up on the beach. A moment later, Kate appeared, walking up the wood-stump steps. "Do you have a minute?"

"I have one or two," I said. "Beer?" It was probably 10 A.M.

"Maybe later." She was still in that yellow bikini, but there was a towel around her waist. I turned a chair to her and she sat down. Her shins were covered in thin patches of mud from the lake-bottom.

"Looks like you've been giving chase."

She looked down and slapped lightly at her legs. Little brown flakes fell off. "I look like this all summer. You writing?"

"Yep!" I waved the notebook in the air manically. "Writing writing!" I stole a glance at her shoulders—brown and spotted—then her hands. They were just girl hands, thin fingers and nails like almond slivers. Hard to imagine them full of frog. "So what is it you two do all day?"

"We catch frogs, sex them, and mark them. Then we let them go."

"Do they like it?" I asked.

"No."

"But it's for their own good." She squinted her eyes at me because I was trying to be funny, but the sentiment was true. Nature hadn't made animals like frogs with the ability to distinguish between when they were about to be eaten and when they were just going to be sexed and marked. "What are the secret-agent headsets for?"

"Have you ever seen a frog?"

"I'm pretty sure I have."

"They have huge tympana—those are the eardrums, the big circles on the sides of their heads. Their ears are even larger than elephants', relatively speaking."

"Okay," I said.

"Anyway, they're attuned to certain frequencies, like the beating of a dragonfly's wings or the buzzing of a fly. We try not to make much noise in the field, since some of the frequencies of the human voice are like those of insects or predators. We just whisper to each other over a radio channel."

"Coming in under the radar."

"Kinda," she said. "Look, uh, we wanted to ask you something, me and Sylvain. We're going to be here for like another eight days, and all we've got down there is a gas stove and two pots. But we have lots of food. So we were wondering if we could interest you in a swap." She tucked some hair over her ear.

"You want to use my kitchen."

"We cook, you eat our food, and we all have a bit of company."

I'd been eating cereal for supper and the idea of a hot meal was appealing. "Sylvain's *French*, isn't he?"

"Yeah," she said, catching my drift. "But he doesn't cook. I cook."

"Are you two . . ."

"We used to be." She picked some invisible lint off her towel. When she looked up, she pointed her eyes away. "To be honest with you," she said, "having another person around would be kind of good for us. You know, make things seem normal."

"They're not normal?"

"They are for me," she said.

That first night, they came in around seven o'clock, lugging their huge cooler into the cabin. That they would unpack their groceries into my fridge had not been discussed, but I was pleased by what I saw. Vacuum-packed bags of frozen meat and fish, frozen tetrapacks of corn, spinach, and strawberries, fresh mushrooms, milk and cream, bacon, eggs, and butter. A rucksack on Sylvain's back disgorged whole wheat bread, pasta, coffee, and corn chips. It was half their provisions; the other half would be delivered after the fifth day. We weren't that remote, but the ministry apparently wanted them to focus on their work. Someone else could do the shopping.

Kate was putting things in the fridge and freezer. "What have you been eating?"

"Just light things," I said. "I eat light."

"I think you've been living on Rice Krispies."

"I have potatoes, too. And apples."

"You need meat," she said.

"Potatoes have protein," said Sylvain, and we both looked at him. He was setting the table. "They do."

"Whatever," said Kate.

I was relegated to a chair as the two of them commandeered the kitchen. I hadn't seen either of them wash their hands, but I wasn't going to make an issue out of it. When I had been alive enough to cook, I wasn't bad. There had even been a time in my life when I made pizza dough from scratch. But when I'd been with J— she'd been the cook. I had the traditional male role: chopping, tasting, complimenting. Complimenting was very important. Sylvain was a little more useful than I was. He was cutting the mushrooms and holding one of the frozen meat packs under his arm to thaw it. It was still in its bag.

I filled three glasses with ice and poured us all scotch. I knew instinctively that Kate drank scotch, but when she took it and rolled the liquor around the ice and then let a bit of it fall into her mouth, that was the first thing. That was the thing you always look back on and you think, yes, that was it.

Kate took the meat from Sylvain and opened it, then cut it into slices. "Venison Stroganoff," she said. There was no cognac, so she poured the rest of her scotch into the skillet. She put on a pot of water to boil the noodles and in about half an hour it was all ready. I'd never eaten venison before. It seemed somehow disrespectful to take a creature like that out of the forest, antlers and all, and poach it in cheap liquor. But it was delicious all the same.

"Why do you keep looking at your watch?" I asked Sylvain when we were done. All through the meal he kept glancing outside and then looking at his watch. It was one of those heavy watches you could swim with underwater as well as calibrate stuff. We'd had scotch with dinner, too.

"I have to finish every day with a count," he said, "and

the count has to start at the same sun-time every day. That's whatever time I did it yesterday minus eight minutes."

"The sun sets a little earlier every day," Kate said. "So they start calling a bit earlier, too. Go on out with him, you two can do it together. I'll clean up."

Sylvain stood—the wild was about to start calling—and waited for me. I made a murmuring sound that suggested maybe I wasn't entitled to such a wonderful experience as standing out in the water at dusk with a heavily pierced Frenchman, but Kate started shooing us away from the table. So I went outside with Sylvain, when all I really wanted was the sensual pleasure of being passed wet dishes and drying them while talking about this and that. I looked back and saw Kate through the window above the sink, not aware she was being watched, and I imagined that after I saw Sylvain off to wherever he lived I would be going back up to the cabin and we'd sit down on the couch and Kate would put her feet in my lap while she read a novel. Afterwards, we'd talk about the novel and she'd be really smart about it, although not intellectual, and then she'd say, "Let's go to bed, babe, long day tomorrow."

"Hold this," said Sylvain. It was a clipboard with a pencil tucked in at the top. There was a list of frogs on it: *Bullfrog, Green, Mink, Northern Leopard, Pickerel, Spring Peeper, Western Chorus.* We were down on the little grey beach. "I say a name and you make a tick-mark. That's all."

"Okay."

He stood completely still. I realized that the fact of the frogs' calling wasn't to help lead him to where they were in the failing light: he was just going to count them by *sound*. This was impressive. To me, the sounds along the lake-edge were without distinction. It was a general commotion, high and low sounds mixing together, repeating sounds flowering up over singular sounds. It was a hubbub and a buzz and nothing stood out of it for me.

"Pickerel," said Sylvain.

"Just one?"

"We can't talk right now. Green. Mink. Take my watch and tell me when exactly ten minutes is up. Another green. Bull."

I started dashing the marks onto the page. At first the pickerels were winning, but then they went pretty much head-to-head with the northern leopards. The spring peepers and western choruses were no-shows. Sylvain stood there as tensed as a pointer and spat out the names. I wondered when Kate had fallen in love with him. It wasn't when he was leaning into the frog-filled dusk, his ear turned slightly toward the water, croaking the names of his prey.

"Northern," he said.

"You sure that wasn't a pickerel?" I said. "Just joking."

When we were done, he took the list away from me and tilted it into the light from the cottage as it gave up its secrets to him. He nodded a couple of times. "Are you interested in this?"

"Sure," I said.

"Last year, we did this lake and two others nearby, and the pickerel and northern leopard populations were lower by twenty-five per cent. Can you guess what that means?"

"They were quieter then?"

He smiled. He surprised himself by doing it; he wasn't expecting that I'd be anything but a drag. "That could be," he said. "But it probably means that the predator population has dropped off in this area. Snakes and herons, some kinds of fish. Maybe they overfed and went elsewhere, or maybe there was a die-off. More pollution in the water."

"Why wouldn't that affect the frogs?"

"It would, but then so would the reduction in the predator groups. We don't really know what causes these fluctuations. That's why we're studying them."

What I didn't like about Sylvain at this particular moment was that I was starting to think he was a pretty decent guy. To care like this. I'd learned by experience plenty of times that there's no vig in judging people too early. Doing that had landed me with J—. Mere attraction can get the better of you and it usually does. "So, will the increase in these kinds of frogs bring back the snakes and fish?" I said, trying to stay on his wavelength.

"If that's the reason why their numbers are increasing, then maybe. That'll be a question we come out here with next year."

"You and Kate?"

He shrugged; that wasn't the point. "Whoever the ministry sends."

Kate's voice came over the ridge just then. It was saying *coffee* and something else, so we started walking back up. "It probably won't be me and Kate," Sylvain said. "But you never can tell."

I pinched my lips together and nodded knowingly. I think this gesture started in the movies and then men all around the world started doing it. It means *you don't have to say another word.*

"Anyway," said Sylvain, and that was the end of it. We came up past the tent, and the tub I'd seen earlier started making sounds again.

"What's in there?"

"Bullfrogs. The big ones go to the lab for blood tests. You know, a three-quarter-pound bullfrog can tell you the ratios of all the various minerals and chemicals in a lake. They're mirror images of the bodies of water they live in. It's actually quite amazing."

I was nodding enthusiastically. Maybe he was a loon. "Then what happens after?"

"Don't worry—they come home. We show the elders the respect they deserve." He smiled at me again.

Kate had made Rice Krispie squares. "I didn't want to deprive you of your evening's ration of cereal," she said. She had piled them onto a plate into a pyramid and they looked exactly like the photo in the Kraft Foods recipe book my mother had when I was a kid.

★

Maybe I'd suffered depression as a child, but I don't remember. How many kids would pass for sane anyway?

Many nights during the worst of it in the city, I'd lain awake in bed and tried to recall if there had been anything really wrong with me as a kid. I supposed that the big difference between then and now was that now I knew what things were called, and I knew what was generally accepted to be normal. As a child, I'd succumbed on a couple of occasions to strange behaviour, and perhaps it had been in line with what children of my generation and demographic were supposed to do. All of childhood is training the animal out of the human—who's to say that the animal doesn't need to manifest these last wild desires? One night I'd run out of the house after some small thwarting—a television show denied, or some insignificant punishment levied—out onto the street, crying and waving my hands around. Neighbours called to me from their front stoops (had I done such a thing more than once?) and I ran past them. I stopped to catch my breath outside of my school and saw my mother turn the corner in her car and come toward me. I ran again, even diving over hedges to keep her from seeing me, and when she drove past she seemed to float by over the street in a bubble of pale light, her face yellowed by the dashboard into a grave frieze of worry.

Another time, a whole summer in fact, I tried to kill animals. I didn't go for the easy ones, like fish, which you could catch on a line and smack with a stick, or even birds, which you could catch with a net if they were feeding on the ground. My prey that summer was squirrels. I figured the match-up was fair: they could run and go right up the sides of trees, and I could throw rocks. They seemed to have a second sight when it came to rocks—they knew to go where the rocks wouldn't. And even when, in rare instances, I made contact, they just shrugged it off. Then I got one. It was eating an apple core on a rock and my own rock caught it there. It tumbled unnaturally off the back and fell into the grass. I went to the rock and looked down, and there it was on its side, some of its ribs sticking out of its fur. And it was breathing, just as it had been when it was eating the apple core. It looked up calmly into the sky for a while, its eye moving back and forth quickly, and then it shook one of its limbs and the eye stopped moving.

I brought it into the house weeping. I told my father it had fallen out of a tree. We buried it and marked the grave and nothing else was said about it.

Maybe I was mad that summer. Or maybe there was more animal left in me than there should have been.

Kate and Sylvain argued that night. Their voices rose to a pitch and then they realized they could be heard and they became quiet again. For a while, there was a lamp on in the tent, and I could see from their shadows that they were sitting as far apart as they could in the pinched space. Then the lamp went out, and Kate appeared, coming up toward the lawn. I returned inside quickly and switched the lights off. She came up below the cabin and spread her sleeping bag on the grass, then slipped herself into it and arranged a pile of clothes under her head. It was a warm night, so she wasn't going to freeze out there. I sat down, worrying that I was seeing their problems as an opportunity. That, I thought, didn't make me a very good person, never mind a good host. But I knew I wouldn't sleep if I didn't go out there.

When she heard my approach, she turned over and shielded her eyes against the porchlight I'd turned on as a sort of signal that I was coming down.

"Are you okay?"

"I'm fine," she said. Her face was a little swollen. "I spent the second half of last summer sleeping outside."

"I can get you another blanket if you want."

She hesitated for a second. Accepting something for herself alone would mean that she was having a separate relationship with me. This I understood: to that point, it had been a relationship with both of them. "That would be great," she said. "And maybe a pillow."

I went in and gathered what she needed, then came down with the whiskey. She sat up and drank a little and we passed the bottle back and forth.

"Are you *okay* okay?"

"Don't worry about us," she said. "We'll be fine. He just has to accept it, is all."

"You've known each other for a long time."

"We were in the same program. He doesn't look the part, but he's amazingly dedicated. He'd do this all year if the lakes didn't freeze." She looked over her shoulder down to the top of the tent and her face changed. "I don't *want* to hurt him."

"I understand."

"But I can't force myself. I mean, to feel something I don't."

I drank. I had the unpleasant sensation that my simple listening was a form of falsehood. Most men have this instinct. Watching her talk, I was filled with tenderness for her, for the trouble she was willing to invite into her life. "Well," I said, "if he can accept what you're offering, it sounds like he'll have a good friend."

"He will," she said resolutely. She put the cap back on the bottle. "You're kind to let us invade your privacy here. I'm sure this is no good for your writing."

"Anything can help," I said. "It's impossible to know in advance what might unlock you."

"Is this unlocking you?" She lay down and put her arms up under her head. In certain books and movies, that would have been my cue. But excruciating experience had taught me that women's come-on lines were never what men thought they would be.

I said, "A little."

"I guess you can't really force that, either."

"You really can't." I collected the bottle off the grass and stood up. "Goodnight then," I said.

I lay in bed after that, and felt her presence out there on the grass. I couldn't have drunk myself unconscious if I'd wanted to. I got up around three in the morning and went back out into the front room to look at her, but she was gone and the light in the tent was back on. The two of them were unable to leave it alone, this relationship that wanted to devour them.

In the morning, I felt uneven. I took my spiked coffee and went out to my spot. Kate and Sylvain were nowhere to be seen, already on the survey's schedule. I took out my two lines of poetry, lonesome lines with no source and no destination, and I experimented with them, removing various words to see if anything about the lines was absolute, inevitable.

of the elements:
human limbs, months, and hours

quadrabalance of human limbs,
and months

quadrabalance of the elements
human months and hours

human elements

This turned out to be a distressing exercise, since it seemed to me that all the lines that were left by these mechanical amputations were all better than the ones I'd sweated so hard to create from will. It started to seem as if poetry followed natural laws that perhaps I had once known, but that now were an alien algebra to me.

Probably Sylvain, with his training in the systems of nature, had an innate connection to the very things that had abandoned me. It certainly seemed to me that what he was doing, his head tilted into the night air, was a better lightning rod for the phenomenological world than was the feeble apparatus of my language. In disgust, I wrote *jugorum* in my book, then slammed it shut and went inside.

Since it would still be hours until dinner (how quickly the shape of my days was changing), I gave in to the pull of television, which to that point I'd treated as a piece of furniture. When I switched it on, the signal came through like light cast through a tunnel. There was a cooking show on one channel, an American game show on another. The sound on that channel was as clear as a person standing behind you, even though the picture swayed like a silk curtain. A woman told something of herself to the host. Where she was from and how many children. That was her, that little list of things. Had she always been this happy? Did she do with her life as she had intended? What threads of circumstance saw her born in that town, give birth to those children, end up guessing the names of songs for money? Her image, almost insubstantial, drifted across; she was as fragile as the signals that came down through space carrying her in them.

"Can you even *see* anything?" asked Kate. She was standing in the kitchen.

"Whoops," I said. "I'm taking a break. You want a coffee?"

"Actually, I was coming up to tell you that if you want, in a couple of hours you can come out with me and I'll show you how to catch a frog. Sylvain's offered to make dinner."

"I thought you said he didn't cook."

"He doesn't. But he thinks he owes me something for last night." She tried to make it sound like an amusing side effect of an experience that had left her with pale grey sacs under each eye.

"You went back to the tent," I said.

"I did." She looked out at the lake. There had been a couple of moments like this, when it seemed that she was on the verge of crossing a line with me. But then she said, "If you thought you were the reason someone was unhappy, you'd probably find it hard to walk away. I do."

"Didn't your mom ever tell you it takes two to tango?"

"Dancing's supposed to be fun." Her eyes drifted to the television for a moment, where the ghostly woman was frantically clapping and weeping. I shut it off.

"If you want to talk . . ."

She turned her eyes on me. "If I want to talk, you're a good listener?"

"Yeah. I am."

"Yeah. I'm sure you are, Russell. Maybe later." She turned on one heel and started out. "Come down around four."

She went out. I had an extra minute or two, so I watched her walk all the way down. Being around Kate for even those two days made me wonder if there could be a world where sex and love weren't so gloomy a business. It seemed that somewhere, people were enjoying carnal lives, unencumbered by ineptness or shyness. But I'd never met these people, or been to where they were. I looked at Kate and felt as if she were pulling the scent of that world into this one, where the great unloved might learn to be more at ease with themselves.

I went down at five minutes past four, after washing my face and changing into some shorts. I had no swim trunks; I hadn't intended on swimming while I was up there, and I generally stayed away from water. I met Sylvain on the way up and he scanned my attire with a jaundiced eye. "You'll get those filthy," he said, stopping me on the path.

"It's just dirt. It'll come out."

"She'll laugh at you and call you a city boy."

"I *am* a city boy," I said.

He looked up to the cabin and then back to me. "How long have you been here? Writing your poems."

"Almost a month." Kate had come across to the beach and was looking up at us. I waved to her. Sylvain didn't turn around. "Why?"

"Maybe I'll rent it after you go. See if I have better luck than you."

"At what."

"Getting over something."

"Sylvain!" Kate called, and now he turned around and shielded his eyes. I noticed for the first time that his irises were so dark they could have been black. They were what gave him his permanently wounded look. "Let him come down. You start on dinner."

"You're next," he said and patted me on the shoulder.

Kate stood on the tiny beach and when I got closer she slid her arm in mine and brought me into the water. "Nice get-up," she said. "All you're missing is the metal detector."

"Sylvain warned me you'd laugh at my *ensemble*."

"He was right." We were standing in five-inch deep water now. "What else did he say?"

"Sylvain? He wanted to know if he could rent the cabin after me. To get over you."

She stopped and took back her arm. She had a look on her face that was somewhere between amused and disgusted. "Maybe the two of you could live here after I go and drink whiskey and keen at the moon together. Maybe turn the place into a retreat for broken-hearted men."

"That's an idea."

"You could offer some kind of package deal: a long weekend up here with mementoes of the old girlfriend, all the chocolate you can eat, and then at the end, someone rows you out to the middle of the lake and puts a bullet in your brain. Charge, like, $399."

I narrowed my eyes at her and smiled carefully. "Men don't do the chocolate thing, Kate. That's girls."

"Whatever."

"How come you sound guilty one minute and pissed off the next?"

She started to talk, but it came out as a huff, and then she gestured helplessly toward the cabin. Her hand went up and then flopped down on her thigh with a wet slap. "He thinks I never loved him. I've been with three guys whose last words were that I never loved them. Must be something about me, huh?"

"Maybe you're attracted to the same kind of man."

"Sylvain's line is that I was with him because I felt *sorry* for him."

"He's only saying that."

"When I met him, he was sick, you know that? He was in and out of hospital—and I'll let you in on something, it wasn't for any physical problems, okay? And that was fucking hard! I didn't do it out of pity, I loved him."

"You shouldn't take someone who's in his state too seriously."

"He's always in this state. That's why I'm finished. So he's giving me one last helping for good measure." She waved her hand dismissively. "Anyway, good listener, you came down here to catch a frog."

"We don't have to. I like talking to you."

She walked around me to a clearing on the shore a few feet away where she or Sylvain had pushed back the lakegrass for a spot to sit, and she sat down and draped her arms over her knees. The insides of her elbows gleamed. "He says to me, the Indians have this saying that if you save someone's life, you're responsible for it. How's that for a fucking guilt trip?"

"Of course you're not responsible for it." To this

point, I'd tried to ignore that Kate and Sylvain had a past.
My attraction to her allowed me to discount that the two
of them were probably as inextricably joined to each
other as I had once been to J——, the woman I claimed I
was getting over. That I'd told a white lie about that in
service of not having to tell two strangers that I was trying
to win a footrace with depression made me feel pathetic
now. It made me feel that I'd lost a chance to say
anything of substance to Kate. Now I was in the position
of trying to be sensitive so I'd seem appealing to this
woman who probably wouldn't otherwise have invited a
person like me into her life. But, I told myself, I'm over
it now. I'm ready for someone like Kate. Maybe Sylvain
just got to her too soon. Maybe the timing's perfect for
me, for her. These kinds of thoughts go in circles, and as
long as you stop them before they reach their inevitable
end (where once again the likely decline of everything
you care about features as the main outcome) you can
convince yourself there are things worth living for. Such
conviction, report those who have it, is as good as its
being true. I went and sat down beside her. "What are
you going to do?"

"I don't know. I think I'm going to wait and see." She
pushed her hair back behind her neck and leaned away a
little so she could see me. "He thinks we're attracted to
each other, you and me."

"He would, I guess. Part of his condition."

"Right."

"What did you tell him?"

"I told him I didn't know what *you* were thinking, but *I* thought you were ugly and you smelled bad."

"Did he fall for it?"

"It was hard to convince him you smelled bad." She stood up. "I'm bored talking about relationships now. I'm finished with men. I want to show you how to catch a frog."

"So that's it?"

"For now."

We stood and walked to where there was another concentration of lilypads and reeds. I just wanted to keep on walking until we came around the other side of the lake and could walk back to some road somewhere that would lead away. But I was aware now that I was stepping into a sequence of some kind. Kate unhooked one of the headsets from her bikini strap and put it on me, then slipped her own on. "Can you hear me?" she said.

"I can hear the real you as well as the microphoned you."

"Walk away now, and don't make too much noise. Go on." I reluctantly started off toward the reeds. I didn't want to catch anything that lived in water. "There's a bullfrog in there, about two o'clock from where you are right now. I've already caught her a couple of times, so she's tired. As long as you don't act all clumsy, she'll probably give up without a fight."

"They fight?" I whispered into the headpiece.

"They struggle. Wouldn't you? Keep going."

I walked toward the edge of the lilypads and scanned the water's edge. The feeling I was being visited with was one I hadn't had in some time—that there was something taking shape, ever-so-vaguely, in my future. Maybe that's what my illness had been about: not knowing where I was going, or what to want when I got there. Or maybe, as I suspected at the time and still do, it was about nothing I could possibly understand, except the work of being alive and not being good at it.

"Do you see her?" Kate said quietly into my ear.

"Not yet."

"Maybe she's gone." I continued closer to the edge of the water. I could hear Kate's breathing in my ears. It was like she was a ghost in my mind. "The trick," she said, "is to know they can't see in front of themselves that well. Frogs have great peripheral vision, but if you come at them front on, they don't really notice. That's how snakes get them."

"Maybe that just makes them stupid."

"Good scientific insight, poet-boy." She gave a quiet, scornful laugh. After another moment, though, she said, "What?" and after a moment, I realized she wasn't talking to me. I looked up to where she was and saw Sylvain standing at the edge of the lake. He had a windbreaker on and a duffel bag was on the beach. She went back toward him. "Where are you going?" she said.

She dropped the headset down around her neck as she approached him, and he retreated onto the grass. Her voice was fainter now, his even more so. I made out that he was leaving to go back to the city. His voice became agitated.

". . . that isn't true," she said, tired with pleading her version to him. "You believe what you want then."

He said something else and I heard her say, "Jesus Christ, Sylvain. We're not going to get paid if we don't finish."

I started to walk back toward where they were, not sure what kind of person he might really be, or if she was in any danger. I got a few steps closer and then stopped and turned. There was the frog. It sat, shaded in the cover of the low scrub, looking out serenely into the lake as if daydreaming.

I spoke quietly into the headset. "Kate?"

"Just a second," I heard her say, and then she put her earphones back on. "What is it, Russell?"

"I see something here."

"I'm going to be a while, okay?"

"Do you need any help?"

"No," she said, and she took the headset off again. I imagined her turning her face back to Sylvain, trying, as perhaps she'd been trying all along, to convince him that whatever love she had for him, it still meant *something*. I waited, wondering if she would come back on and instruct me somehow, but I could hear nothing. After a moment, they moved into view closer to the cabin, and I watched them, the discussion their bodies were having, and I saw her take him into her arms. She held him against her, and he let himself be held. That was the kind of embrace it was. Then they vanished from view behind the cabin.

I didn't know then what was required of me, so I kept moving slowly to where Kate's frog was and extended my hand. The animal didn't register me at all, or at least not in a way I understood. I moved forward as slowly as I was able. I knew I'd been taken away from my purpose here, I'd been more than waylaid, but this was as good a reason to be here as any. Letting life come in from the side was a wise thing, I thought. It worked for frogs. Although perhaps they'd settle for a little more of knowing what was right in front of them, in the long, forward view. I was only a couple of feet away now, and the frog turned itself a little to the side, like a mechanical toy. I shifted position as well. I heard a car door shut—it must have been my car—and at that moment, I shot my hand out and tried to grab the thing, but it vaulted into the air, its limbs flailing wildly, and plunged into the water near my foot in a flash of white and green. I felt it brush against me, a glancing of flesh, and then it was gone. I waited a moment to see if it would come up, but it must have known to go somewhere I couldn't see into.

When I got back to the beach, the tent and the rest of their gear was gone. I went into the cabin and looked around, but there was only silence there, and my keys were gone from the bowl on the front table. I took off the headset and lay it in the bowl, where it gave off a faint crackling, still bringing her in, still connecting us. I had a proper appetite now and started cooking. I had some sense of faith as well, but why and in what, I wasn't sure. I was settled in myself for once, and had the feeling that I had done something with my day even though it hadn't been remotely like poetry, and probably it wouldn't be like poetry again.

ACKNOWLEDGEMENTS

"Cold" appeared in *The Notebooks*, Doubleday Canada, and "Split" appeared in the *Queen Street Quarterly*, both in slightly different versions. My gratitude to the editors of those publications.

To Maya Mavjee, Pat Strachan, Ravi Mirchandani, Ellen Levine, Michael Winter, Esta Spalding, and especially Michael Helm and Anne Simard: thank you. "Long Division" is for Tim and Kougar, "Orchards" is for my brother.

ALSO BY MICHAEL REDHILL

Martin Sloane

Jolene Iolas, a student in upstate New York, encounters Martin
Sloane's work while visiting a Toronto gallery. Flush with the con-
fidence of youth, she strikes up a correspondence with the older
artist, and eventually they become lovers. She learns Martin's
story, and cherishes it as her own.

And then, without warning, without a word, he vanishes. There is
no hint of his fate, no chain of cause and effect to be followed.
Ten years pass, and Jolene learns to stops trying to make sense
of what has happened to her. But before she can fully return to
life, the opportunity to confront her ghost arises, when she hears
that someone named Sloane has been exhibiting artworks
identical to Martin's in galleries in Ireland . . .

Seamlessly crafted and beautifully written, *Martin Sloane* evokes
the mysteries of love and art, the weight of history, and what it
means to bear memory for the missing and the dead. This is a
truly remarkable debut.

'It is rare to read a novel that pulses with such pleasure that
you don't want it to end, but this is what Redhill's debut
delivers.'
Independent

'A powerful meditation on the implications of memory and the
vacancies opened up by the loss of love.'
Observer

arrow books

BY SCOTT SPENCER

A Ship Made of Paper

Daniel has returned from New York to the Hudson River town where he grew up. There, along with Kate and her daughter, Ruby, he settles into the kind of secure and comfortable family life he longed for during his emotionally barren childhood. But then he falls helplessly in love with Iris Davenport, the black woman whose son is Ruby's best friend. During a freak October blizzard, Daniel is stranded at Iris's house, and they spend the night together – the beginning of an affair that eventually imperils all their relationships and their view of themselves as essentially good people . . .

'Superbly captures the giddy roller-coaster emotions of infatuation – the self-deceit, desperation and heights of ecstasy are all beautifully conveyed . . . Compassionate and powerful, *A Ship Made of Paper* is a tempestuous, absorbing journey into the human psyche.'
Time Out

'Irresistible . . . This is a book about love as a torrent, a force of nature that overwhelms families, harrows lives and lays waste to whole towns as it thunders through. Love may be our only hope, but when you put this book down – not an easy thing to do – you may wonder how civilisation survives it.'
Time

'Scott Spencer is a magnificent writer'
Anne Tyler

arrow books

BY ELISE BLACKWELL

Hunger

Travelling to the world's remote places, a daring scientist has spent his life collecting rare plants for the Soviet Union's premier botanical institute. Even at home with the wife he reveres, his memory brims with the beautiful women and luscious foods he has known in exotic climes.

But when German troops surround Leningrad in the fall of 1941, he too becomes a captive of the city. With food supplies dwindling, residents strip bark from trees, barter priceless antiques for bread, and trade sex for sugar. In the bleakest hours of the hunger winter, the institute's scientists make a pact: no matter how desperate conditions become, they will protect the precious cache of seeds that is their country's future.

'Perfectly judged, beautifully executed . . . Blackwell's style is to weave together, with elegant lucidity, bright threads of narrative, historical snapshots and digressions, and enigmatic poetic reflections and asides . . . *Hunger* has been called harrowing, but it is also uplifting. It comes back again and again to the human being's ability to surprise himself, or surprise another, or to be surprised.'
Daily Telegraph

'Harrowing . . . Blackwell's stark novel is fascinating for its study of how human behavior shifts when faced with the most extreme circumstances and when motivated by fear . . . insightful and gripping.'
San Francisco Chronicle

arrow books